# ALL THE NIGHT GONE

A NOVEL BY SABRINA USWAK

Stonehouse Publishing Inc. is an independent publishing house, incorporated in 2014.

Cover design and layout by Anne Brown.
Printed in Canada

Stonehouse Publishing would like to thank and acknowledge the support of the Alberta Government funding for the arts, through the Alberta Media Fund.

National Library of Canada Cataloguing in Publication Data
Sabrina Uswak
All the Night Gone
Novel
ISBN 978-1-988754-28-4

Disclaimer: *This is a work of fiction. Names, characters, businesses, places, events and incidents are either the product of the author's imagination, or used in a fictious matter. Any resemblance is purely coincidental.*

*For Workshop C, Dr. Allyson Stack, and Silvia*

*Thank you*

—

The 7 is nearly empty now. Three A.M. sees only certain kind of traffic. By the time we've crossed into Saskatchewan, the sky is endless, the land table flat. There is only the semi heading east, gas sloshing in its giant containers. One other colourless car passes by in the descending dark, heading elsewhere.

When the rain starts, sticking to the windows like glue beads, the radio is playing a song that will soon be *that* song. The one which compresses infinity in a single note; that will trigger a heavy sadness in my chest if I hear it later.

The road is straight and disappears into a pinprick.

It is silent but for the song. We've not said anything since passing Teo Lakes—a scattered silvered mirror. Charlie's stopped jiggling his leg. I can see his knuckles moon-white on the stick-shift. The truck's too small for him. So's Three Hills.

Maybe that's why Dill left. Being in a place too small with a sky so big. Hills that gleam in the hot dry summer wind, endless to the horizon. *An illusion of opportunity*, Charlie said once.

Dill hadn't said anything.

We'd tumbled out of bed and she was gone. Room sparse.

Her window was left open. Always. Air curled, rippling through the sheer curtains, raised like dissolving flags. The sky was dusty blue, bleached with a smear of clouds. Charlie stood at the foot of her empty bed, jeans faded and ripped, t-shirt rolled over the crowns of his shoulder bones. Silent. I stayed in the doorway, hands at my sides as he lifted the bed by its end and tossed it against the wall; the wood cracked like summer thunder.

***

She's got a wild laugh, Dill. Starts low and ends high. Sometimes it trills, sometimes it is silent. *You have a range of laughter when it's been tested*, she said.

Dill likes fall and spring. Transition seasons. *In October and April the days are mirages of two seasons, depending on which eye you close.* When I told her I liked fall best because of all the colour, she said: *Don't fallen leaves smell like nostalgia for summer green, Ben? That's why fall feels familiar. It's a new phase with the memory of the old. Like us.* She'd looked out the window then. We were in May's café. I remember the smell of coffee. Months ago, now. She kept running her thumb over the handle of her mug.

*When fall comes, it's like the arrival of an old friend.*

***

It's been nearly four hours since we left home, over twelve since Dill took what was left of home with her.

*You'll have to go far*, May told us. Out of Alberta, definitely. Off the highway. Head north once you've gotten near to Saskatoon. There is a road that follows a river, winter cold. You'll follow it too. It's probably full of all kinds of run-off, so don't you think of drinking it. Go careful, it isn't a paved road. People don't use it much. Watch for the reeds lining the river when it disappears from view. It will veer sharply and the road'll narrow into an even smaller one that's just twisting pebbled mud. *I don't have to tell you to slow down.* Soon enough it'll straighten out again. It is, after all, Saskatchewan. You'll pass a clump of trees, those lonely handfuls of green you sometimes see even on a bare plain.

You'll come to the houses. There'll be a barbed-wire fence so you'll have to get out of the truck. There's no point in waiting for someone to open it because they won't. They'll have seen the dust trail behind your truck long before you see them. The houses are set on a hill. All three of them. Sand-brown with fingers of smoke reaching out of dented chimney stumps. There's nothing dotting the land except for stones piled in clumps the shape of a man with his arms held out. There will be people there. Not many, but enough. They won't look at you kindly but at least you'll be met in the eyes. You can ask them about Dill. Maybe you'll learn something. Might be you'll just get up to those doors and lose your nerve. Or someone'll herd you off before you've ducked under the fence. Maybe you'll realize that it's none of your business. Could be you just think her name and that it was enough to have gotten this far.

***

Dill.

Who came one day and took off another but left echoes of her laugh in the house and newer impressions of feet in the carpet; who found the covered tracks of Charlie's smile under his anger-mask and laughed her laugh until he used them again, his mouth livening white, remembering how.

# —

I have drifted off. I realize when my head, weightless, angles to my chest and my neck snaps it back. Opening my eyes is a struggle. I blink away the reach of sleep. Charlie grips the wheel so tight I can see every vein raised on the back of his hands. Rain drums constant on the roof of the truck. My throat feels full of wool. I rub my eyes until they burn.

"Charlie, we need to pull over. You need to sleep."

Electric green numbers read 3:45. A muscle pulses in his jaw. I recognize its rhythm. He keeps silent, staring. In the dark his eyes are hollowed out. Our headlights sputter a couple of metres ahead. Everything ink black. At the two A.M. mark I managed to convince him to keep the radio on so we wouldn't drift off.

*They only play garbage on the radio this time of night*—his grudging response.

He didn't wake me. It's something Mom would let me do. I sit up straighter, energy flickering automatic in my joints. A faint electric feel.

He hasn't said anything scathing about the music. I don't even think he hears it now. Maybe he doesn't want to. Even I can admit that it's growing on me, making me think. Charlie would say that's probably because I can be such a girl sometimes. Dill would just let it wash over her. She's not wary of letting the mind run, like me and Charlie. She says it leads us to places we're supposed to find.

"Charlie, c'mon. It's not worth driving in the rain anyhow."

The windshield wipers thud and scrape. Thud. Thud. Whee.

He keeps staring into the pitch-dark, rain breaking against the windshield in glistening rivulets.

I curl my hand into a fist and relax it. I do this twice.

"Is it. Are you—are you mad at me?"

My voice cracks. At Charlie's silence I turn to face the passenger window. Can barely see my outline, hologramic against the glass. I pretend it doesn't matter what he says.

Charlie tightens his fingers again on the steering wheel, skin and leather squeaking.

"Charlie?"

The song on the radio is the new alternative rock song everyone sings to at school. It moves into a bridge filled with cellos and smashing drums that shimmer in my ears. The truck swells with sound and it makes me hold my breath. I want to shake my brother.

"No, Ben, I'm not mad at you."

The width of his hands strangle the wheel. His knuckles ridged in reflected light.

"Okay."

He sags a little into the driver's seat.

I have to choose my words carefully. Anything can set Charlie off sometimes. But it's too late in the night; it's past the hour of holding back, of stepping lightly. I think I read that somewhere once.

"Is it what May said?"

He grinds his teeth, glancing at me. He really does look tired. Like he's been hiding how tired he's been since—well. Since then.

"Yeah, I guess."

"I think she was just—"

"Trying to be an unhelpful bitch?"

"—trying to do right by Dill."

Charlie lets out a laugh. It is short and hoarse.

"Yeah. By giving us a bunch of cryptic directions to some place by a river in Saskatchewan we're supposed to find. Following a road with no name."

We'd stared at the map as if it could show us where. It just stared back at us in a snarl of lines and blue and green patches. Full of names of places. Swift Current. North Battleford. Kindersley.

"By saying that we should just leave Dill alone."

I look at my hands. Longer than Charlie's, thinner. *Instrument hands.* I curl my fingers.

All the anger goes out of Charlie. I can't look at the lines in his face. I stare at the rain, white static illuminated by the headlights.

I think of the night before she left: yesterday. Me, grinning at Charlie's red face after he swallowed too much chilli sauce. I try to seek out the plan in her eyes—some kind of cue we missed when we were all laughing over dinner. Tucking her hair behind her ear more than once. Stirfry with rice—her favourite. Had it meant something? The last supper. I shred the memory apart until it is just a handful of images I can recall by rote, not the one settled in my chest, kept by the pumping blood there.

"She didn't say anything, Charlie. Nothing."

"I know."

The radio broadcaster is murmuring in his deep voice but too quietly for me to make out the words. A timpani rumbles a distant storm before piano trickles a new melody, low and light. I am discovering I like alternative rock and feel okay about it.

"Who is this band?"

"The hell if I know."

Charlie's pretty exclusive with his love of blues and thrash metal, but he loves King above all else. I hear him howling through Charlie's door some nights: *I'm gonna change my ways, I'm gonna move to the deep blue sea.*

When I come by the shop Charlie's always listening to the radio. News, talk-shows, music, whatever. Usually radio from other provinces. The one time we learned about fishing disputes out East; I followed along quietly as Charlie worked on and on, coveralled knees showing under a red car. I was imagining fleets of boats as large as icebergs floating crews of men all speaking different languages, waiting and waiting, before racing to haul every unblinking fish onto grey decks. The cold spray of the Atlantic not enough to stop the pulling and heaving. All the cod. Seeing upside down trees of nets glittering with fish. *Emptied the sea right to the root*, a woman said to the news anchor. All of the resignation and rage in her voice. Charlie from under the body of the car: *That is fucked up*.

I hate the pop stuff they play on a loop in DQ, so I tend to want just anything else. Silence over the radio; the radio over Dad's old records. Usually I just read to fill my head with words.

Silence looms again. I grasp at the first thought to keep Charlie talking. We'd been driving in near total silence since turning out of Three Hills.

"How come Dimitri was pissed?" I ask.

Charlie cracks his back, rolls his shoulders. I can feel the hulk of his body, all crowded muscle, stretching out and seeming languid. I'd seen Dimitri's red face and Charlie's barely reined-in anger: like a silent movie, muffled from inside the waiting truck—their long and furious argument had varied in pitch whenever other mechanics walked by. All of it conducted by their moving arms, up and down, side to side. Sound alive when Charlie slammed into the truck. His heavy breathing, clattering keys. Needing a moment before he started the engine. I knew not to ask about it then.

"Dimitri's being an idiot."

I roll my shoulders.

"Guess he had to make it look like it mattered. You're reliable."

They'd only shrugged when I said I needed some time off. DQ. *Damn Questionable food*, Dill called it. *Don't Question*. It made it hard to take drive-thru orders without wanting to laugh. I remember my first night there: standing behind the counter with that stupid visor on and other boys from school coming in after hockey practice. The big one, Max. Looking at me contemptuously, angrily. *Gave you the job out of pity, did they?* I remember staring straight back at him, bored by it all, knowing I couldn't lose the job. Seeing Charlie's relieved face over and over when I told him I'd got it. Informing Max and the three big idiots behind him it was probably because I had more than half a brain, which qualified me over him. Watching his face flush with embarrassment, feeling a twinge of pride and shame that I'd mentioned his losing the job to his friends.

Knowing they'd come back for me later.

And did they. My hand absently passed over my ribs. I remember locking the store up and hearing boots crunch on the snow behind me. Someone wiping their nose, cracking their knuckles. Feeling a thrill, a mad desire for it—wanting the blood in my mouth.

*Fucking pussy. Nice uniform, asshole. Where's your brother now?*

But Charlie had come. Came around the back when I hadn't met him right away. The fists and feet stilling suddenly, my head spinning and split lip burning on the snow. Spitting out a glob of blood. Charlie hadn't said anything, didn't have to. The other boys ran while Max stood defiantly.

*You can't do anything otherwise*—Charlie grabbed him by the front of his jacket, lifted him easily, just looked him in the eye. *Otherwise what?* He'd asked quietly, a promise dark in his throat. He slung me over his back and we were silent all the way home. I didn't say a word to him—just limped into my room and shut the door. He'd stood outside it for a bit, his breathing soft. For a while we stood, listening to each other not say a word. He finally left to go lie on the couch. I could hear the springs compress even from my room.

"I'm pissed at her." Charlie says quietly. "Just up and gone. Like we never meant—that maybe it was all just—"

I hear the clack of his teeth as he chops the sentence in two.

We. Him and her? Or him and me to her?

He turns on the hazard lights, slowing the truck. The rain sounds softer now, like it's dripping from a watering can onto tile. Red flickers into the night. The lights make a metered ticking noise that join the windshield wipers.

Tick tick. Thud. Thud. Whee.

"Let's forget popping the tent in the bed tonight, okay, Ben? I'm too tired and everything will get wet besides."

"Sure."

With the car turned off it is quiet enough to hear our breathing, the rush of rain on windows. We pull our sleeping bags over us. A huge semi roars by, red lights ridging its back in points. I think of a dragon pushing out of its cave, opening its mighty jaws. The truck buckles in the hurl of wind, lit orange for a moment. It is soon silent again. I can feel the vastness of the sky through the roof of the truck, can close my eyes and see Venus white and bright. The little dipper next to the big one, fixed in a rotation that can see the whole world.

"Charlie?"

"Yeah."

"Maybe something came up and she didn't know how to tell us."

"Maybe."

I can tell he can't talk about Dill anymore.

Sleep sinks heavy on my limbs, having waited patiently. I gladly close my eyes and see Dill smiling, teeth gleaming. Her long hands running through her hair, each nail pearl smooth. Charlie's mouth relaxing around its edges as she gestures wildly, telling a story. Lightly touching her waist when he walks by her cooking something on the stove.

Just me and her. Looking across the table: her leaning her face against her fist, pizza cooling on the plate. Picking at the crust. *What do you want after high school, Ben?*

I morph her face into summer nights out on the porch—everything gold and green and faded. Dad barbecuing steaks, the grill hissing and spitting. Punch-pink sunset.

My stomach rumbles loud enough to hear. We haven't eaten since that rank meatball sandwich from the gas station hours ago.

I shuffle in my sleeping bag, pulling back the memory of Charlie hovering at Dad's hip, standing on his tiptoes to get a look at the electric red coals. Mom's laugh floating through the screen door, newly fixed with a white trim—turpentine sharp in the nostrils whenever we passed through to go outside—telling Charlie *pull up your pants*. Rhubarb pie hot and tangy in my throat. Taber corn glistening with butter and salt, leaving yellow puddles on my blue-chequered plate.

***

What did we talk about at dinner? I don't remember. I want to. I squint until my face is pinched from trying to grasp from the recess of memory. Voices are always at the fringes—murmuring, whispering. I can never make them speak louder. It's like trying to hear every conversation in an airport terminal at once, feeling like your skull will split from the volume of ricocheting noise.

I only have snapshots of conversations, phrases, a word. It's all muddled now by things I want to imagine were said.

—

Her engine light had been on for ages but it finally gave out.

She ran her long fingers through her hair. A nervous gesture, we'd learn later. Just made it into Dimitri's car lot. She drove a rusty blue Toyota Corolla, the back fender falling off. She had a duffel bag with a broken zipper. Straight black hair to her shoulder-blades. Cheek bones sharp under her eyes.

*Not my doing*, she said, when I told her she was pretty, my ears burning.

I could feel Charlie rolling his eyes. She laughed her laugh. It startled out of her throat. Bugs were summer dust in the waning sun. Her eyes gleamed black.

"Excuse my brother, he's an embarrassment."

I flipped Charlie off.

Dill began fidgeting with her car keys. They clinked quietly, reminding me of the wind chimes on our porch.

"How long will it take to fix?"

Charlie ducked under the hood.

"At first glance I'd say your car's completely shot. But I'll need to take a closer look to be certain. You'll probably need a new one."

He looked back at her, hands resting on the flaking lip of the car hood. She was rolling the keys over her knuckles. Clink clink. Tension hummed around her. Me and Charlie shared a look. He closed the hood. The sound made her startle.

"Do you want to call someone?" I asked.

Her lips tightened into a half smile, but she didn't say anything;

just stared at the quiet shell of her car, headlights grey behind the frosted glass. She looked like she wanted to kick it.

I glanced at her backseat. A baseball bat was hidden under the passenger seat. Charlie saw it too.

"Is there somewhere you have to be?"

"No, I just—well, I hadn't planned to stop. Not here."

Her eyes flickered in the direction of the highway; headlights streamed in gold white ribbons.

"Hard to plan for cars breaking down," Charlie said.

She laughed again and nodded.

"True."

"There's a Super 8 if you need to crash. And Dimitri's got a couple of cheap used cars out back you can take a look at," I said.

"I don't have that kind of money."

We all fell silent.

"Are you sure there's no one you can call?" I asked.

She shook her head. For a moment her hands trembled as she ran them through her hair again.

I saw the decision in the ridge of my brother's spine.

"It's okay," Charlie said.

***

We'd all clambered into Charlie's truck and drove back to our place. All the windows were black, the house a blue outline in the moonlight. The street was quiet, even Mrs. Shelly's yappy dog that lived next door. Like the town was holding its breath. I tried not to glance at her in the rear-view mirror.

Charlie had to throw his weight into the door for it to open. It swung and dangled uneven off its hinges.

"Keep meaning to fix that," he muttered.

Dill stared: our shoes piled against the corner of the entrance way, no mat. Mud and dirt smeared and dried on the floor. The sliding closet mirror-doors covering a few coats and a handful of empty hangers.

We moved into the hallway with its trampled brown carpet,

small and bare of anything except a large fist-sized hole in the drywall. Dill lingered near it before turning away. There was a faint outline of where a shelf used to be. Her hand moved as if to trace it but stopped at her side. The paint had watered from heavy cream into pale beige. I thought I saw her look at Charlie but her eyes gave away nothing. She pushed the strap of her duffel bag higher up her arm.

With the three of us in the hallway it was crowded and I realized I'd forgotten it could be. I bumped into her and as she turned, her elbow hit Charlie. We all apologised at the same time. Dill laughed. The sound cut through the stale air. Charlie's face relaxed, finally exhaling. He rubbed his hand against the back of his neck. His ears were red.

"This way," Charlie pointed.

The kitchen: small and square with an old chequered linoleum floor. Her eyes swept across the oak cabinets, the fridge with no magnets or pictures; some empty cardboard boxes of microwave dinners on the counter, half a loaf of bread. I noticed an empty six-pack of Pilsner that had been sitting for a few days on the small dining table. Dirty dishes in the sink. Next, we shuffled to the bathroom. I stood outside since we all couldn't fit. She glanced into the medicine cabinet with no door and nearly empty toothpaste tubes. Shaving cream and shaver. Two toothbrushes. One box of painkillers. Charlie explained the trick of turning on the shower. A ring of rust around the drain. When he stood, wiping his hands on his jeans, she leaned forward and twisted the neck of the showerhead tighter with a deft crank and then gave it a jerk, turning the tap. Water came out uninterrupted. Charlie stared at her. I'd never seen that expression on his face. She shrugged.

I flattened against the wall when she stepped back out into the hallway. She paused. The door to my room was open enough to see inside.

"A lot of books in there." Her voice warm.

When we got to the small living room, she visibly relaxed. Cozy with its well-worn green couch, heavy blue wool blanket, and photos lined on the mantelpiece. She secured her duffel bag behind her to carefully look over each photo, as if she was memorizing them, brushing some dust off a few of the frames. She paused in front of one for a long moment, head slightly bowed. Some of her hair slipped over her shoulder. We didn't move or say anything. Charlie was in the doorway. I could hear his weight shift over the old wooden floorboards. I thought he cleared his throat to say something, but he didn't. I stood awkwardly behind the couch, picking at the soft material. Dill didn't notice.

"You two are so young in this photo."

She glanced over her shoulder at us, amusement softening her mouth. For a moment she seemed older. I guessed she was around Charlie's age. He could do that exact expression she was doing, that shift between humour to seriousness. Barely nineteen. It was the way she carried herself: a nervous energy that only just fit her limbs. Charlie had the same thing, that careless grace.

It was the photo of me and Charlie with ice-cream smiles in front of the tiger cage at the Calgary Zoo. Our eyes half moons against hot sun. Dad had been telling a joke. *What do you get when*—she was holding the photo in her hand. She held it up so she could see both us and the picture. Dust snowed from the frame onto the carpet. I watched her smile crease. She traced the edge before placing it gently back down on the mantle.

"You look like your parents. Especially your father. But you both have your mother's eyes." She turned from the fireplace.

There was something in her voice. I kept picking at the couch. It seemed important to not look at her directly. When the floor creaked I turned to find her standing in front of Charlie, waiting. They were staring at each other.

"Your room's the empty one at the end of the hall," Charlie said after a while, leaving the room.

She watched him go.

I cleared my throat. "Here, I'll show you."

I stayed in the hall as she placed her small bag with its broken zipper into the empty room. Her eyes swept over the faded picture stains on the walls, the impression of a large bed left in four neat circles on the carpet. A feel of dust. She opened the window. It creaked. Cool air filled the room. It was soft though; summer night air. She looked for a moment outside at the small backyard, curtained in black and blue. I wondered if she could see the bushes gone wild, fistfuls of dandelions like bouquets of tiny suns crowding the grass. She turned, arm resting on the windowsill, finding small divots of a standing wardrobe, a round chair. The empty closet with bare hangers, doors thrown open, smelling faintly of dust and lemon and wood varnish. A drawn quality to her face, an expression of something I recognized. She gave me a smile. A sad one.

Charlie was dragging his futon through the hallway, the noise filling the house. I pressed against the wall next to the door and felt the material brush past my knees. He didn't look at me as he passed into the room. He mostly slept on the couch. Dill stayed by the window. She wouldn't know he'd given up his bed until the next morning.

The square white mattress emphasized the room's bareness. It dropped with a decisive thump. We all stared at it instead of each other.

"I'll get you some side tables and a dresser and stuff," Charlie said, after a beat.

"You really don't have to go all that trouble."

Charlie shrugged. "We got some stuff packed in the garage."

He wiped a bead of sweat off his forehead, I hovered in the doorway. I couldn't move past it into the room—not for a year. Charlie could though. Sometimes I'd see him lying on the floor, arms folded behind his head, staring at the ceiling.

She looked at the futon and then the both of us, hands tucked against her elbows. Her duffel bag was so small.

"You can stay as long as you want," Charlie said.

—

Sun wakes me in a riot of red and pink and orange. Canola gleams yellow to the horizon. Passing cars are flying bullets over the highway, dewy from last night's rain, quickly drying. The truck heaves with the traffic. All the windows are fogged. My skin feels cold and filmy. Charlie's still asleep. I study his face. His arms are crossed. He doesn't move when I poke him in the arm, so I shake him, hard. He blinks slowly, glancing at me, dazed. Goosebumps upraised along his forearms. I find old newspaper under the seat and push some into his hands. We scrape the emptiness of the land back into view with every swipe of newspaper; the blood-bowl sky surrounding us on all sides now.

Charlie gets out to take a leak.

When he gets back and turns the key, the engine grumbles into life. I stretch and feel bones pop. Electric green numbers flicker 7:35. The radio blinks on and Charlie finds a rock station. Queen's *Fat Bottomed Girls* fills the truck. Charlie shoots me a grin I am already returning. He blares it as I buckle my seatbelt and we roll down the windows and shout the whole thing to the wind, throats raw, looking at each other mid head-bang, me gesturing a shapely girl in the air while he holds his fist out to the sky, laughing, laughing, passing a large green sign with white letters posting Saskatoon, 312km, the sun outlining Charlie all in red-gold light and warming my face.

***

We pull-over where a dusty and peeling gas station hunches. A diner sits in a feeble angle of blue shade. I smell canola oil and bacon grease and hear our stomachs growl like a lion's reproach, deep in the throat.

The engine sputters and radio blips off mid lyric.

"I'm starving."

"Me too." Charlie unbuckles his seatbelt.

"We okay for gas?"

"Yeah, just under a half a tank. I brought two extra jerry cans in the back. We'll put some more in at the next stop."

"Just two?"

Charlie gives me a look.

"I don't know if you've noticed, Ben, but we're kind of winging this whole thing."

I roll my shoulders.

***

When Charlie threw Dill's bed into the wall and it clattered to the floor I could only say, *We should check May's*. I had to get him out of the room. Because. Otherwise. Well. I turned from the cracked bed frame and Charlie didn't say a word. Followed me out. Turned the truck on. The sky was the kind of blue that made you think of the sea. *I'm gonna change my ways, I'm gonna move to the deep blue sea.* It was already warm. People were out and about no more no less than usual. Charlie didn't go over the speed limit and I didn't tell him to hurry. We didn't look at each other. I think I said something stupid like, *maybe May needed Dill to stay with her because of the sleepwalking*. Even though May hasn't needed anyone since 1979, so she says, especially on Canada Day when she's completely sauced.

The café was busy. May looked like she expected us there. It gave me a sinking feeling. She loudly told Mrs. Shelly to *Wait a damn second, it's not like you need the sugar or caffeine anyway.*

She said Dill had left because *Something had happened*. Her face accusing. Charlie's hands were loosely clasped, elbows on his knees. He was staring at the floor tiles, winded. I asked *Where* to keep her talking.

She'd given Dill her car and some money for gas. *And a small bite too because Good Lord that girl eats like a bird.* I asked where she went, again. While straightening her beaded bracelets, May said: *Might be that place in no-where Saskatchewan—you know, where she comes from.* The deep lines around her mouth folded, pinched tight as if pulled from a drawstring. She looked out the window, bright with sun. *Might be she went somewhere else though. Didn't say.*

I never thought May could miss anyone, let alone a girl she only knew for about a year. But then May never had any children or husband or anything and I guess you can never really know what will make people have that sad expression; the one that makes the skin on their face look heavy. Or what will make people give away their car and hard-earned money and just hope that everything turns out for the best—even though they're the one in the rear-view mirror along with the dust.

We drove back home in silence, then sat in the driveway staring at the peeling grey paint of the garage door.

*She won't come back unless we go to look*, I said, certain.

Charlie still, tight-lipped. Then, after nearly fifteen minutes: *I have to go to work first.*

***

A bell jangles as we enter the restaurant. It looks preserved from another time: old movie posters and chrome counter edges with speckled linoleum. The smell of oil and grease is stronger. Coffee too. I can see a jukebox, yellowed and silver in the corner. Pride keeps the floors clean, I think. It's a place Mom and Dad would like. I rub my hands against my jeans, clammy all of a sudden.

The restaurant reminds me of a place we all went to once, coming back from one of many rain-filled camping trips. We all traipsed in puddles and the fake leather booths squeaked from our wet rain gear, which we had to peel off. Dad said Mom looked like that fish we never caught and she told him if he intended on getting home by car he should rethink the comparison. They chuckled while the waitress set down glasses of orange juice; me and Charlie buried behind the menus. He was muttering *pancakes* over and over, while I felt water squish between my socks, and considered having a side of sausage and back bacon.

I don't remember much about that particular trip except it rained the whole time we were there and Dad still thought it was a great opportunity to show us how to fish. We learned I was better at gutting them than Charlie, who looked faintly green when it was his turn to try. Determined to outdo me, he doggedly gut every fish we caught. He couldn't even look at them later, let alone eat them when it was time for dinner. I suspect that's why he doesn't like fish now. Mom enjoyed being in the tent with her coffee thermos.

That's what those memories smell like now. Instant coffee, wet earth, fried fish. The sounds: rain on tent canvas, dripping between leaves and laughter.

Remembering gives me a tight feeling in my chest. Dill would know. She'd ask me to tell her what I was thinking about.

I look at Charlie and put my hands in my pockets.

The booths in this diner are the same cardinal red. Me and Charlie scuff our shoes on the dusty entrance mat. There are a handful of empty booths along the back wall and window and a couple of single stools at the counter shaped like mushrooms with matching faded red cushions on top. Fresh Saskatoon berry pie sits warm on a glass stand. A cherry one too. Nestled between them a sign that says "A La Mode $1." Another on a music stand: "Please Seat Yourself." The mirror behind the cashier makes the place look larger, more crowded.

Charlie goes for a corner booth next to the window and I follow, still looking around. He sits so that his back is to the room, unfolding a menu. He's got a deep line between his eyebrows. When his forehead did that Dill would smooth it out with her thumb. The first time it caught him so off-guard he flinched, face flushed. She didn't look bothered though.

Makes me think of when Dill asked me what the biggest difference between me and Charlie was. She was in my room, (a habit she'd started even though she'd been living with us just two weeks) and not embarrassed at all from asking such a direct question. She'd been with us long enough to know Charlie left early, came home late, and then fell asleep on the couch, sometimes with the T.V. flickering a montage of colour over his hunched shoulders. That I stayed in my room to read or left to go for long walks.

Dill had got a job working for May and would do other odd ones like babysit or walk Mrs. Shelly's dog.

She'd stop by my room every day. To ask me things. It was startling because I'd find her looking at my bookshelves or sitting patiently cross-legged on my bed. I didn't know how to answer at first. But then I'd be walking home quicker after work without realizing, brimming. When she asked me about Charlie I remember saying *I think our differences are pretty obvious*, and she said:

*I mean something that's like drawing a line in the sand different. There're differences like looks and mood and interests, but then there're the ones that really mean something. That tell more about the person.*

She stood a few feet away, her eyes black. Three inches taller than me. I remember my room, blurred green from sun framed between the leaves of the poplar outside my window. When I answered, my voice was far away, an echo down a well. I told her that I say they died, Charlie says they're gone. She put her hand on my arm and didn't move it until the front door slammed and Charlie's footfalls sounded through the kitchen. I asked her if she had any siblings and her unreadable expression came back.

*No.*

I asked, *What's different between you and your closest thing to a sibling, then*? She frowned. I thought she wasn't going to answer. Then her teeth flashed, distracting me from something glinting in her eye—maybe. Tucking her hair behind her ear, no piercing holes, I noticed.

*She says that chances are always there for us to take and I say they're given to us, if we're lucky.*

***

Charlie snaps the menu shut. I realize I've been picking at a loose thread in the seam of my jeans and stop.

"The full breakfast is definitely the best deal. With a side of pancakes and a coffee, it'll be ace."

"Those pancakes do look good," I say, glancing over at an old couple quietly eating. Every now and again they gaze across their plates, warmth in their faces.

I decide on a Coke instead of coffee because I can't quite get into coffee even though it smells good. It seems like one of those things I'll eventually start to drink out of necessity one day, like whisky.

We sit for a bit and don't say anything. I fiddle with the ketchup. There's some crusted around the lid of the bottle. It's one of the glass ones that make it difficult to get out the ketchup even when you tip it over and shake it vigorously.

"I like this place," Charlie says after a while.

"Yeah. It's like those diners Dad always took us to after camping."

Charlie absently pushes the salt shaker. Some dusts onto the table. "Yeah."

I can't remember Dad complaining or getting moody about the rain. Only the once when we left a particular deluge and the sun came out just as we got in the car to drive home and he swore for a full ten minutes, to Charlie and mine's delight. Mom didn't say anything because she was trying to hold in her I-told-you-so-this-happens-every-time expression.

I look outside. The parking lot is mostly gravel, two lonely gas pumps, and bulrushes in the ditches by the turn-off. Our battered truck stands beside a gleaming black motorcycle and small beige VW camper van. A wooden flatbed truck with an engine block strapped tight slowly pulls into the lot.

"He always insisted on tenting. 'More fresh air that way, boys.' 'What's a little water and mud, dear?'" A laugh comes out of my chest. "Maybe if he got one of those pop-up roof campers like that one, we'd—"

"Ben."

The muscle in Charlie's jaw is jumping. From the side he looks like Dad. I wonder if he notices.

He's still determinedly staring outside. We have to angle our legs away from each other because we're too tall to sit knee to knee. The booths are small. They used to feel large when we were younger. I rub my hands on my jeans, which are too big; an old pair of Charlie's.

I'm more like Dad in temperament.

Mom felt things with explosive energy while Dad was quiet. Charlie and Mom would yell at the T.V. screen about whatever thing was happening. Me and Dad would just share a look—like whenever there was a righteous speech from one of the lawyers on *Law & Order*—there are so many, and usually in raised monotones. We'd have a game to see who'd smirk first. Mom and Charlie recreating the theme song while we had our silent battle of wills.

We'd always give in at the same time. Dad's eyes would fold in the corners like raised blinds and I'd be smiling so hard my cheeks felt stiff after.

I clear my throat. "I think they'd like this place too."

Charlie flinches. It's subtle. His hands folded on the table jerk a little. "Just order one side, okay?"

"How much did we bring, anyway?"

Charlie glances briefly out of the corner of his eye at the other patrons who are not listening.

"About a hundred."

"A hundred?"

"Shh."

"That's it?"

He looks at me, eye-to-eye, serious.

"We couldn't bring it all, Ben."

"Obviously—I'm not an idiot—"

"Well then—"

"But I remember there being a good-sized pile. There was definitely enough to bring more than a hundred bucks. What about that bit I added from last week? You had that extra from that last-minute fix-up you did—for that rich guy who kept insisting even after you'd closed shop."

Charlie runs his hand through his short hair. It makes it stick up. He won't look at me. "Look, it should be enough, alright?"

Something flares in my gut and tastes bitter. "We have to drive north of Saskatoon, for fuck's sake. Who knows how far. We'll eat up that extra gas and then some."

"It's all we could spare."

"That'll barely be enough to get to this place and back home and maybe, you know, have something to eat in between."

Charlie flattens his hands against the table. "Dill took some of the money, alright?"

"What can I get you boys?"

I turn automatically towards the voice, a buzzing in my head. The waitress is soft and pear-shaped, with copper curls pinned and pulled into a low ponytail. She's wearing a faded grey t-shirt with a giant dreamcatcher. Dill has a similar one.

"The full breakfast with a Coke and a side of pancakes, please," I say, dazed.

"The same, coffee to drink," Charlie mutters.

She smiles. Her teeth are uneven and small, but warm folds crease around her eyes, which are green like the colour of a lake we drove past to Radium Hot Springs one summer. Olive Lake. Surrounded by pines as tall as giants.

She takes our menus.

When she's gone I clear my throat. The back of my neck is hot. I can't look at Charlie so I look at the table. I can see those careful piles under the floorboard in Charlie's room with Dill placing her small share in Charlie's hand, so he could add it for groceries.

"What do you mean, she took some?"

Charlie rubs his face again. The tired expression is back. I want to shake him.

"I brought what I thought we could spare."

He resumes staring out the window. I can't read the expression on his face.

"Why would she—she wouldn't do that. Charlie—"

The hotness from my neck has spread to my ears. I take a deep breath, think of Dill, and my thoughts stutter. I just see her hand placing bills in Charlie's, their fingers touching.

"Charlie, what do you mean she took some?"

"Just—forget about it, Ben."

"Forget about it?" My voice cracks.

The diner goes quiet. A man with a long black ponytail and worn motorcycle boots shifts on one of the bar, which squeaks.

I lower in my seat. A flush creeps up Charlie's neck.

His anger. I feel it coming off him as an invisible force.

"Drop it, okay?"

A trickle of something moves along my spine. I taste blood at the back of my mouth, my bones stiffening. Like the fight behind DQ.

"Why didn't you tell me earlier?"

He swivels to face me, eyes so dark they seem to absorb all the sunlight. The brooding expression. I want him to stop doing that. He hasn't since—well, then.

"You can tell me that stuff. I'm not a kid anymore, Charlie."

I study the linoleum table top, the glare of sun in it. Each coloured speck.

"I guess I couldn't really believe it." He exhales, looking away again.

"When did you know she took the money?"

He rests his elbows on the table. I feel it. The feather-light brush of panic.

"Was it before you went to the shop? Is that why—"

"Ben."

I sag, glance at our idle dusty black truck.

Concentrate on it.

Dirt rims the truck tires in a spoked wheel shape. Bug guts smeared in green and yellow sunbursts dappling the windshield. I start tapping my fingers on the table, a mixed rhythm of the songs I vaguely remember from last night. The rumbling timpani.

I realize that Dill never said where she was from, except *Sas-*

*katchewan. Someplace too small*, with a laugh that covered something else.

Coffee and a Coke are set in front of us.

"The food'll be up in about five." The waitress gives us another friendly smile before disappearing into the kitchen.

Charlie sits perfectly still with his hands rolled into fists. The ice in the Coke clinks gently against the sea-green glass. The coffee steams. I can see that muscle moving again in his cheek.

Maybe he's thinking about the same thing I am. The unsaid things. Or what little we have for directions.

"But how much did she take?"

A stool scraping over the floor interrupts Charlie's response. The man with the long black ponytail has risen to stand. His boots are steel-toed silver, black. His face impassive, carved as if out of weathered wood. A faded tattoo of a woman curves over his forearm. He meets my gaze straight on, eyes robin-egg blue. Only when the door to the diner shuts do I shiver.

Charlie shifts, leans forward, his knees giving off heat. I can tell he wants to hit me.

"Ben, I'm not going to ask again."

Forks and knives clatter. The waitress is placing dishes in front of us. I stare blankly at them.

"Syrup, ketchup, salt and pepper are all on the table. If you need anything else just give me a shout."

She is turning around when I feel the question rise up out of my chest.

"Excuse me, ma'am?"

She turns back.

"Yes m'dear?"

"We are looking for a friend of ours. Her name is Dill. She's got long black hair that goes to the middle of her back and a nice laugh. She's driving a white hatchback. Have you seen anyone like that? She'd have been by recently."

The woman shakes her head kindly.

"I'm sorry, sweetheart, haven't seen anybody like that. She

sounds lovely."

I'm nodding before I can stop. I feel lightheaded. From hunger. Yes.

"She's kind of our only family now."

The woman's arm moves as if she means to touch my shoulder. A faint bell ringing from the hissing and steaming kitchen snaps her hand back. She looks at us as if to gather us in, green eyes clear and bright.

"I'm sorry." She hurries back into the kitchen.

The food smells so good my stomach hurts. I grip the fork. The metal feels cool in my palm. I realize I'm sweating and grinding my teeth. I won't look at Charlie but I can feel him looking at me.

"Ben."

I start cutting my pancakes in half and then half again.

"Ben."

Charlie's voice is firm but not unkind. It rumbles out of his throat and reminds me so much of Dad's that I startle. I grip the fork tighter. A pressure begins to build against my heart like something's gushing and I realize tears are dripping down my face. I pretend I don't notice and take a bite of the pancakes even though my throat has swollen. The pancakes are fluffy and melt in my cheeks but feel like sponge as I try to swallow, expanding to stay lodged against my Adam's apple.

I pour syrup over the rest and spill some onto my eggs and bacon and toast and potatoes and watch as it slowly coats and curls over the plate like a quiet wake following some sea-beast. Water wavers on my eyelids warping my vision like blown glass, throwing the table into a blurred prism of colour and light.

"Ben."

Charlie says my name in a whisper. I know he hates it when I cry and I hate it too so I don't. I haven't since it happened but I can't help it now.

"Hey."

A strong hand grips my wrist. I study the bones and veins and jagged scar on the thumb and feel the calluses and warmth. The grip tightens.

I wipe my nose with the back of my other hand and look at Charlie, whose eyes are glistening too.

"Yeah, okay."

He ducks his head in relief and takes a moment before letting go of my wrist.

—

We were home watching T.V. when it happened. Road accident. Loose gravel, going too fast. The car spun out of control, careened off the road, and landed on its rusty top, dust billowing from under it, flooding into wheat fields; the sun a rounded eye, staring red.

*Died instantly*, Jimmy said, taking off his black aviator sunglasses. *I'm sorry*. Sweat gathering under his cop hat, running down his temple.

I had been standing behind Charlie's tanned and freckled arm. Noticing each tiny hair tipped in gold, the tightened cables of his muscles. Speechless, still. Thinking: happy graduation, welcome to adulthood.

I watched the tick in his jaw start that wouldn't go away, his hands curl into fists that wouldn't relax, that would obsess over the guts of cars after smashing punching bags when people weren't around to warrant it. Watched as my older brother just became older, clenching grief between his shoulders so it could turn into anger and then he'd have the energy to carry it. Guardian Charlie. Who had to separate himself from just Charlie and brother Charlie.

But it all got tangled. Guardian Charlie who'd finished high-school and wanted me to finish too, with honours. Just Charlie who got drunk after graduation and set a car on fire. Who stood barely three feet away from it and held his arms wide open against the towering flame, laughing and laughing into the black night until Jimmy pulled him away, the squad car's light stuttering blue and red. Letting it go because Mom and Dad's service had been the day before but grabbing him by the collar and telling him to get his shit together otherwise I'd be put into the system. Brother Charlie who tore all the pictures and paintings off the walls as I yelled at him to *stop, just stop*; tossing furniture into the garage—the comfy plaid chair with the broken footrest handle, the green wool blankets, Dad's jackets, the baseball mitts, Mom's red leather shoes and silk scarves—all of it in lumpy cardboard boxes; the funny fruit magnets and ski-boots and postcards from the Okanagan; the tattered cookbooks and muffin tins—all of it piled in the stuffy dark.

***

After it happened, me and Charlie had this new way of looking at each other as if the other were a mirror. Brother. Guardian. Minor. Charlie won't talk about what happened. I don't know when he will. If at all. I just keep all I want to say in a well that's going to overflow and someday there won't be any way to stop it.

When I came back to school in the fall after it happened, people didn't know what to say; which was fine, since I didn't really know what to say either and I mostly kept to myself before anyway, so why stop? I remember we were studying *Of Mice and Men* in English class. Everyone asleep except for the few girls at the front diligently taking notes. I was in the back corner and couldn't concentrate on anything except for the line where George says, "If I was alone I could live so easy." I remember standing up and walking out of class past all the turning faces, the teacher lowering her arm from the dusty chalkboard. All the way to the auto shop.

Dimitri got Charlie who exploded when he saw me and asked why the hell wasn't I in class, but I wouldn't move or say anything because I couldn't get out the words. He was holding me by the collar of my shirt, dragging me back outside into the bronze autumn sun but all I could think was that I would be what holds Charlie back. That maybe that's what he thinks when he looks at me.

He couldn't go to the States for university. He had a partial scholarship for boxing. I remember when he got that letter in the mail, he put a hand over his face and was laughing and crying and Dad whooped, and then Mom let us have some beer with dinner. He grabbed me in a headlock and gave me a noogie as I told him *Stop it* and he said, *You can come visit me kicking ass in the USA, Ben.*

I remember he hung up the flag with the school letters on his door. It's under my bed now. I found it crumpled in the garage underneath Dad's golf shoes.

***

Charlie dragged me all the way back to school. To the front doors. Held me by the front of my shirt and said, *you have to go to school, Ben. I need you to go to school, okay?* And then he turned away and his voice went weird so all I said was, *Okay,* to his retreating back.

—

We are quiet for the rest of breakfast and leave a good tip.

The truck is stuffy. It is going to be a hot day, I think. We roll down the windows as we get back onto the highway. Air ruffles through my hair like light fingers. Long ones. I steer the comparison away and let my concentration drift.

—

I'm looking at the map again trying to guess where the turn-off might be. A ways still to go. Roads and lakes seem familiar now after staring at them so long but are still useless in two dimension. *A road that follows a river.*

"We could drive into Saskatoon and ask somebody?"

"Like any city idiot would know the place."

I stuff the map back into the door compartment.

"Probably have to get off the highway sooner than we think," I mutter.

Charlie shrugs.

I stare out again into the oncoming road, at how little there is between towns. A few homesteads or grain silos. Mostly flatland with some dips and rises. Gleaming ponds. The odd herd of cattle. Only one or two cows glancing up at the sound of our engine. What do they think about while grazing? Noticing the ones who look up were usually a ways away from the others. I imagine the steady calm of their gaze, their long eyelashes. And suddenly we'd cross through a town—a four-way stop, the speed dropping to 50—and you could sense most of the town was within arm's reach. I re-saw the railroad tracks following the highway. Gas stations, Co-Op, diners. Yellow school buses parked in lots with RVs and work utility vehicles. Motels with names like Motor Town Inn or Heartland Rose Inn. The odd discoloured building with a flat overhang and four wooden posts to tie horses. Relics from frontier days.

Charlie fiddles with the radio. He chooses an AM station with thready reception. The voices are quiet, faraway enough to be from another time; talking in even tones about a crisis. A female announcer interrupts with weather updates.

"It looks like today will be a hot one: temperatures staying in the high twenties throughout central and southern Saskatchewan. Remember to stay hydrated and—"

A sudden shudder from under the hood of the truck.

"What the—" Charlie releases the clutch as the sound gets louder. Some kind of grumbling whine. He herds the truck into a pullover. With the ignition off I can hear the wind in the grass and distant motors from surrounding farms.

We get out and I stretch to crack my back and wrists and arms and fingers until Charlie gives me a look of mild disgust before ducking under the hood. I turn to gaze around.

There is some kind of general store and longhouse with a row of motorcycles out front. I scuff my shoes on the dirt and start pacing in slow circles.

If she took some of the money, then it's because there was a reason and the reason enough to make her leave. What was it? And couldn't she say? But then. What must it have been like—driving on her own all that time with a bag with no zipper and a baseball bat. Sky and wind for company. Going and going across roads under dissolving clouds. Knowing whatever happens, happens, and it's just you.

Had she planned to stay?

I think Dill is stronger than we are and that's what really scares Charlie. And if I'm honest, me too, because, without being needed—what do we offer? What makes a person stay? And even that isn't enough. You want people to want to.

Now I'm thinking about a time I should bury deep enough until it becomes a dream or fiction; something to keep locked away. Unallowed to float to the surface and change the way I look at her and Charlie or the way they look at me. But.

But what about when she came to my room and Charlie wasn't home and she was going to tell me something important about herself? I could tell. I looked over my book because she had stilled, even her breath; the weight of what she wanted to say a presence in the room, filling her to the brim. She said, *Ben,* and I knew I'd never looked that directly into somebody's eyes before, so close that the rest of your vision is all indistinct but you know you see everything, and I wanted to say, *it's fine, it's fine. All of it.*

She was closer than she was earlier and I hadn't looked at her face so closely, never dared. The chapped pale of her mouth and freckle on the mound of her cheek and I thought maybe if—maybe if—but even that thought startled the moment. It must have been on my face. And suddenly a magpie was at the window screeching, giving us a start, her hand was in my hair—no, my hand had drifted to her hair—

A shadow angles over my path. Steel-toed boots. I glance up leather motorcycle chaps, a gleaming silver belt buckle, worn shirt under a vest, tarnished thumb ring, dark ponytail, and a curving woman tattooed across a scarred forearm. A man with eyes almost too bright for his face.

"Howdy."

I nod.

"Where you all from?" Jutting his chin out towards my brother.

"Three Hills," I say, automatically.

Charlie's head snaps up over the hood.

"I went there once, to the college."

"Oh?"

"It was a long time ago."

He keeps staring at me like he's carefully peeling back every layer until he can see what he needs. Charlie slamming the hood makes no difference. The man doesn't move or look away. I study the fading blue outline of his tattooed woman. Pin up body; dress a watery bruise. I try to decipher the initials underneath her round thigh.

"Ben." Charlie's voice digs into the nape of my neck.

"Well, we're just making a brief stop." I turn to where my brother's standing.

"You all looking for someone?"

Fear sinks down my back. Charlie remembers himself.

"What makes you ask?"

"We're just taking a drive—haven't ever been around here," I say, at the same time.

"Is that so?" The man smiles.

He is one of those people who knows violence; who's known it all his life.

Charlie knows this too because he has dug his feet into a wide stance, crossing his arms to look bigger. "Yeah, it is."

I'm distantly glad I double-knotted my laces.

"Well, I could have sworn you all might be at your wit's end."

"We're just fine." Each syllable hissing through Charlie's teeth.

I shift towards the truck door but the man's hand darts out to latch onto the handle. Charlie stills, just at the front tires. Recognizing something about this situation; his face unreadable from the angle of the sun. Sweat starts under my arms.

"It might be you may need some directions from people around here. You go on in that way, well, they won't be too kind in answering you."

I can smell metal and grit in his breath. Menthol. I don't move and take shallow breaths. I will Charlie not to move, knowing this man wouldn't hesitate.

"If I could make one small recommendation," he leans closer, so his voice can run right through the blood vessels of my inner ear, fingers tips light against my collarbone, "I wouldn't go on talking about one's finances around some of these places. You just never know who might hear."

He swivels, boots grinding the dust. I sag into the door. More men who look weathered and tattooed file out to light cigarettes.

When we're in our seats rolling up the windows, I hear him call out, "Good luck with finding her."

—

An explanation should be enough. To see something and say, that is the reason for her kindness, for his sadness, for their silence. Why she left; how they died.

I don't think anyone would want to be able to hold all the competing truths of the world in the palms of their hands. I think it would be frightening—a fear that left you with few options.

But just a simple reason for why—it should be enough.

***

When I think of when Jimmy told Charlie and I how "it" happened—*they were going too fast*—it's not out of the ordinary, is it? To go too fast. Not on these roads. But the look on Charlie's face, adding it all together—the things you are meant to be careful of when you are young, always *be careful* and *watch yourself* and *think think* but all the while feeling invincible, immune to the idea of *what if*, of what it is to grow older, to know you have to be careful. Enraged at having to learn it now, this way. The look of incredulity on his face; pained at how simple this explanation was, how obvious, how preventable. *Going too fast.* Witnessing a new kind of change start in him and trying to stop it by saying,

*Charlie it's—*

But he knew what I was going to say. That I wanted to explain what happened another way but the explanation was already there and simple enough: *going too fast*—and silenced me with a look I could name, and then smashed his fist through the entrance wall.

And Jimmy, standing politely, holding his hat as if it was a prop. The hole flaking plaster dust. The gleam of sun and hills through the slit of open door nearly painted it was so still. I looked down at our entrance mat with its cursive "Welcome" and said, *Thank you for telling us, Jimmy*, and didn't understand the feeling in my chest because it felt like laughter and it felt like rage, and closed the door.

***

I started going for long walks; first to where it happened. I felt nothing but disappointment at the barrenness of it all—just fence and field and road. A short cut. Nothing special, nothing to stand out. Maybe it was the scenic route. I don't even remember where it was they were going or coming from.

*A fucking waste*, Charlie kept repeating, under his breath at the service. Vibrating next to me, curling and uncurling his fists. My dress shirt wrinkling, too big and starting to itch. I had this compulsion to grab his hand but we'd grown way past that stuff. I wished for anger then, too. Rather than this hollow yawn that had started to swallow everything at the bottom of my chest and would keep going until nothing was left. But when he raised his hand to his eyes I dared—reaching out and grabbing his free wrist, squeezing, and we stood like that for the rest of the words and when it was time to let go I felt a part of my brother go too.

—

Something sprawls ahead in the shoulder of the road. A shadowed boulder. Charlie steps on the brakes immediately and puts on the hazard lights. We haven't spoken since the incident and the air in the truck is oxygenless.

A dead deer.

It's a small one. Red, smeared like paint, has dried to brown chalk, outlining it.

"No one's moved it yet?" Charlie asks, angrily.

He pulls the truck over and turns off the engine. Hazard lights ticking, ticking. He's already unbuckled his seatbelt. He grabs a pair of work mitts from under his seat and puts them on.

I get out of the truck too.

The heat outside is dry and moves off the grass in breaths. Road and sky meet in the far distance and the land seems to go on and on. Flat. Upturned wheat and rolls of golden hay dotted to the horizon. Power pole wires disappearing into faint pencil smears.

We move alongside the shoulder until we get to the animal.

I clear my throat. It's difficult to look at. Red and pink and purple and white fur swim in front of me. I blink and it's like being handed a crimescene photograph too much in focus.

I turn away when Charlie gently puts his hands under the body and the neck lolls back. I walk through the grass up to the fence lining the highway. I can see a concave barn; old, ash grey, roof folded into an x. A small oil pump moves up and down slowly next to it. I stare at the motion until I feel rhythm steady in my chest, breathing deep.

When I used to think about dying, it was always "what would it be like?" and "how would I want it to happen, or, not?" If it's a dark night and I'm being honest with things you don't speak about, dying would be a reunion with Mom and Dad and it sounds like a blessed relief, but it also seems like this force you don't get to understand or anticipate or choose.

And if I go, if I went—what about Charlie?

Charlie's too mad to die. Wants to survive at all costs as a flip-off to what took our parents. But I think there are times he wants to just fall asleep and not get up for a long time. Right after it happened he looked so still when he slept, I always shook him awake to check. It took a while for his eyes to flicker open and when they did, he wouldn't move for a minute.

Me and Charlie have to live for one another. Otherwise, there is nothing. I get that. I don't live for Three Hills or school or just because. I do for Charlie. And it's not something that means if he was gone I wouldn't because then, where would the proof be that our family ever existed? Where would all the memories go? There'd be no one to gather them in, to hold on, even though they keep leaking all over, too fast for me to grab.

When Charlie threw everything in the garage I started taking back as much as I could. Choosing things slowly, night by night. Dad's jacket, the worn leather one. I'd held it up to my nose first and it smelled like him. It was a punch to the chest; it felt like waking up from something I didn't realize was making me shut down. The second thing was a necklace of Mom's, a silver Celtic cross on a long chain.

I put as much stuff as I could fit under my bed, in my closet; between books and figurines and photos on my bookshelf. Like preparing my own personal bomb shelter or museum. All the evidence. All the flotsam and jetsam of our life with them.

Charlie says Mom and Dad are gone. I guess it's because they can't come back and thinking that makes it easier for him, but that's impossible because they only died. All of it is still here—wells and wells of it—all in the veins, and I wish he'd just allow it to be what keeps us going, not something that's bloodletting from the inside.

When Dill came it was only a couple of days before the first year anniversary since it happened and it was this thing in the room in the morning that just came unannounced, even though we knew it had been a long time coming and we couldn't even look at each other.

Do we put on a suit? Do I get flowers? Do we tell this stranger in the house? Do we go to the grave? What time? When we found out about it or when we feel like it? What is the right response for these things?

And Charlie didn't know and I didn't either and it was the first time he looked visibly helpless since being Guardian Charlie, so when we were sitting around the breakfast table looking at our cereal (Dill the only one who finished) I said, *Let's go after this.*

And he looked relieved and put his face in his hands and Dill sat still because all of this was raw. She was witnessing something she wasn't meant to, but there it was, and she said *There are some prairie lilies in the garden outside.* And because she'd figured out what was unsaid and knew what to say, and about Mom's favourite flower, it just made sense that she would go on staying with us.

As we were getting in the truck she handed me a fistful of orange petals, like holding a prairie sunset, and said, *I'll be here when you get back*, iron in her voice.

***

"Hey."

Charlie's standing next to me. We stare out at the flatland, gold and green. The horizon this huge eyelid you could stare into and not see a wink. I absently rub the back of my neck.

Charlie cracks his back. "Ready?"

"Yeah."

We walk back to the truck. Out of the corner of my eye I can see tips of fur bleaching in the sun. Long grass around the deer obscures most of what happened to it. From this angle, it could just be sleeping.

***

I don't know what happened to make Dill go suddenly. I feel like there's something I'm missing, but all the conversations I've had with Dill seem to have clashed into one another and I can't keep them still to figure which one was the significant one, which one was the foreshadowing moment. I can't figure out if it was there all along or something really did *just* happen. I don't know why she took the money. It's like trying to understand how there can be two conflicting answers to a question and both are right. It had to have been an emergency. But then, why wouldn't she say anything? Did she think we wouldn't believe her? Wouldn't listen?

When we got back from visiting the cemetery, she'd made a massive amount of food. Me and Charlie came into the kitchen in our wrinkled sports coats and she'd made a pie and a roast and steamed vegetables and rice and soup; all this random stuff, and she was standing in the middle of the kitchen looking like she'd never stop cooking; baking powder all over the surfaces, carrot skins making criss-cross shapes over the grid-patterned linoleum floor. She was stirring a pot so vigorously that we surprised her. She clasped a hand over her chest and we all looked at each other and started to laugh, honestly, and she started crying at the same time and I never found out why and maybe that's where all this could've been figured out, but I never thought to remember and ask.

—

In the approaching distance is a wall of cars, bumper to bumper. We have to slow to a crawl. Air coming from outside is oven dry. Everything stretched and starched. I feel sweat on the back of my shirt. The sun is high, glistening bright like a coin in water.

Charlie cranes his head out the driver window.

"What's this?" I say, as we nose up behind a small blue sedan with bikes on the roof.

Charlie turns on the radio and scans for a station.

"Road repair, maybe."

Static buzzes. He tries to find the AM station that does constant traffic and weather condition reports. A man's voice blips on.

"There has been a major collision on Highway 7 stopping all eastbound traffic. Ambulances and police are on the scene. No other information has been given at this time but expect delays."

"Shit," Charlie says.

I turn the dial to another station. Classical. Another. French. I turn the radio off.

Charlie adjusts in his seat and leans his elbow against the open window, face resting in his palm. I can hear grasshoppers vibrating in the grass.

I reach into the side compartment of the passenger door and take out the map. We are not far from Saskatoon. I look at the patterns of blue, different lakes and rivers, wonder which is the one we're to follow. It's probably too small to be on the map.

"We should put gas in now," I say. "Since we're going to be parked for a bit."

"Yeah."

Charlie shuts off the engine and turns on the hazard lights. He gets out of the truck and I hear pebbles scrape under his shoes as he goes to the back. The truck jolts a bit as he drops the tailgate and climbs in. I glance out the rear-view mirror at him. He picks up a red jerry can. The cars in front of us still haven't moved. I can see a couple talking through the shaded back window of the blue sedan. They look young, newlyweds maybe. She's resting her elbow on the driver's seat, her fingers playing with the hair at the nape of his neck. Like when I walked into the kitchen and Dill was raised on her feet and Charlie was holding her elbows and their faces were bowed into one another's.

I get out of the truck.

Sun burns the top of my head. I stand next to Charlie. The smell of gas, sour and potent, fills my nose. Charlie twists the cap back on.

"I was thinking we should turn off on one of the smaller roads before we get too close to Saskatoon," I say.

Charlie gets back into the truck bed. His brows are furrowed. "Why?"

I hold my forearm in front of my face to block the sun.

"We're supposed to head north once we're near Saskatoon, remember?"

I follow him as he walks to the back and hops off. He brushes his hands onto his jeans.

"Which one?"

"What?"

"Which road should we turn on?"

I shrug. "I'm thinking just get as close as possible to the outskirts. Maybe to the first ring-road. Turn before then."

Charlie nods.

"Excuse me—"

We turn. A middle-aged woman is standing behind us. A teal minivan has pulled behind the truck, hazard lights flashing.

"Do you know what's going on?"

"Accident," I say.

"Oh, dear. Well, thank you."

She turns to go back to her van. I can see two boys craning their heads from the backseat. The oldest one is giving a fierce stare under a mop of black hair. I wave. The youngest waves back. The two of them start to shove at one another until the woman gets in the van. I can see her leaning around the seat.

*Stop it, you two, we're almost there. Just wait a little longer.*

I frown.

"Ben?"

"Yeah. Coming."

We turn back to the truck. I scuff some pebbles into the grass alongside the shoulder. When we get in, I glance at Charlie. He's grabbed the map off my seat, and is scanning it.

"Remember that trip we took with Mom? To Banff?"

I leave the passenger door open for more air to move through. A breeze kicks dust off the dash.

Charlie doesn't reply. I stretch out my legs, knee-joints cracking. The mountains: giant and ice grey; Moraine Lake a turquoise blue and green. Images scatter across my mind as if someone dropped an envelope full of photos. Canoeing with some woman who had a throaty laugh, Charlie dragging his paddle through jade waters, reflecting a bright orange hull, lifting it to spray me. The smell of weeds in water. Mom staring at a phone on the wall, her face in her hand.

"We stayed with her friend...I can't remember her name. She laughed a lot. Dad couldn't come with us."

Paper rustles.

"That was a long time ago."

I look at him. Burrowed into the map. Not like he's reading it, though. Just staring a hole right through.

"Came to me, is all."

I lean back in the seat. Study my fingers. There's something about the memory. Maybe it's because the whole thing is in blue-scale and I remember stress-lines around Mom's eyes. Something tightens in my chest. I rub my forehead, staring at the small rose at the top of the blue sedan's license plate.

"We stayed there for a while and that woman took us out canoeing a lot. What—"

"Just forget about it, Ben."

The couple in front of us kiss.

I roll my hands into fists so the veins resemble the river lines on the map. Dill would tell me to describe more about the woman with the laugh. Ask about Mom. *Dill took some of the money, alright?*

Silence wells. The sedan inches ahead. Charlie puts the map on the dashboard and turns on the engine. We creep forwards. Saskatchewan reflects upside down in the windshield.

I watch as a crow swoops onto the barbwire fence next to the road. The only dark thing in the landscape. I study the curve of its beak and beady eye, cocked towards me.

Charlie likes birds. Fixed one up once that had a broken wing. With string and popsicle sticks. A cardinal. I remember it lay still for him while he fastened the string around the makeshift splint. He told me I had to be still too if I wanted to watch, so I wouldn't scare it. Mom got really mad since he didn't wear gloves when he did it.

*It could be carrying diseases.*

Charlie told her he didn't care if he got sick just so long as the bird was okay. I think I was six. Charlie must've been ten. I remember wearing a Spiderman sweater I'd gotten for my birthday that year. Red as the cardinal. Dad told her to relax when he got home from work.

*Don't tell me to relax, dear.*

I steer my thoughts from that memory—the sharpness in Mom's voice pinching at my ribs. The crow looks back at me beadily, tilting its head to the side. Asking me a question. Expecting me to ask it one.

We continue forward a bit. The crow's eyes follow. It readjusts its wings. I lean out the passenger window.

"Want to come along? Show us the way?"

I hear Charlie turn in his seat. He doesn't say anything though.

Grass and horizon begin to move by at a walking pace. I see an odd marsh glistening near the road. Reeds reflect in the water's smooth surface. We don't fall back to a standstill.

"That didn't take too long," Charlie mutters.

He turns on the radio again and finds the AM station.

"What appears to have been a four-car collision eastbound on Highway 7 is now being cleared. Three passengers have been airlifted to hospital with serious injuries. There were four fatalities."

Charlie changes the station. Classical. French. He turns it off. He inhales to say something but doesn't. Starts jiggling his knee. Sometimes it brushes against his keys hanging from the ignition. They clink and chime.

Makes me think of when me and him and Dill drove to the Royal Tyrrell Museum. Squished next to Dill, her arm against my arm, her shoulder bumping Charlie's, his knee grazing the keys after every bump. We drove with the windows rolled down while dust billowed in a cloud around the truck so we could smell the approaching storm. Dill told us it was a big one, pointing to the mare's tails on the horizon—like some giant hand had smeared white paint where it meant to finish a picture of horses running. It rained hail big enough to hold in the palm. Charlie picked some up and threw them at me. I pelted him back. We drifted around the museum longer to wait it out, chose which dinosaurs we thought were most badass or ones we liked because of how bizarre they looked. Stood next to a T-Rex skeleton and just stared at it in silence. Ended up driving home in the tail of the storm, slowly. Rain coming in the windows and slicking over our arms and legs—bare since it had been a hot day. I remember Dill's knees bumping into mine, her skin smooth, making me startle. I leaned further into the door.

*Summer storms here are something else.*

Her hand was resting next to Charlie's thigh, their shoulders pressed together.

She had lived with us for a while by then. Long enough that she had pyjamas and a hairbrush and her own toothpaste and was in a photo with us on the fridge. It was around then I saw him glance at her long legs when she was reaching for a mug in the cupboard. When she sat next to him on the couch he wouldn't move his arm if hers was next to his. His eyes seemed to follow her wherever she stood. He'd lean against the counter in May's cafe to talk to her. She'd place her hands on the expanse of his back when looking over his shoulder at something in a shop window. She smiled. He smiled. And smiled. And then, that time. When the lights were off in her room because it was a full moon. Huge. Filled the entire window and made the room a grainy black and white.

They had been sitting on the bed, side by side, backs to the door. His head was bowed against her bare shoulder. She was cradling his face. His arm was behind her waist. They didn't move. I'd held my breath.

I look at the sky now but there's no line of thin white cloud in the distance—a blurred border that can also tell of an approaching thunderstorm. Tonight will be clear, then. Enough to see the stars.

"When do you want to bunk down tonight?" I ask.

Charlie stops jiggling his knee.

"Not sure. Maybe just see how far we get and go from there."

"Are we going to park off the side of the highway again?"

He shrugs. The traffic flow moves a bit faster, going at least 20 clicks now. As we move, flashing lights materialize to Charlie's left. People in yellow picking up orange pylons forming a Y perimeter. We pass a ripped-up husk of a car filled with shattered glass slowly being loaded onto a tow-truck bed. A huge grey pick-up, dented in the front, already sitting on it. Glass and shredded tire are everywhere. Two cars are mashed together. There is wetness on the pavement of the road. I can see red in the windshield of one car and feel something move in my stomach. I close my eyes and lean my head back and breathe deeply. Ringing in my ears.

"Charlie?"

"Yeah."

"Do you—do you see a white-hatchback?"

There is a terrible silence.

"Ben," he says, like he lost the ability to speak for a second.

The dizziness still there. I open my eyes and stare at the grey ceiling of the truck. I see faint stains. Coffee, probably. It makes me close my eyes again.

"Do you see one?" I ask again, through my teeth.

A moment goes by.

"No. None of the cars are white."

"Okay."

We gradually speed up. I lean my head out the open window and hold my breath, hands gripping the side of the truck as wind runs over my face until my lungs burn, then take a deep breath. Dry heat and wheat and grass all in the air I take in. Sun warm on my eyelids. The grey in my chest and stomach recedes.

We drive in silence. I watch the dome of the sky, the bicycles on the roof of the blue sedan in front of us glinting.

—

Right after it happened, there was a week of nothing, and then Charlie would come home tripping drunk, crashing into the walls and slumping into the hallway. Alcohol smell overwhelming, greasy. The worst of it was when I opened my door once to see sweat and blood smeared along the hallway wall where he tripped, and Charlie laying there, slurring to no one:

*All got it comin', them, all goddamn right.*

Not hearing me say, *Charlie, what the fuck*? Not recognizing my voice.

Still muttering *sure, yup the last one, you got it, asswipe.* A small laugh that sounded entirely unlike him. The whole scene distant and reeling. I grabbed him by the wrists and started hauling him to the bathroom so he could lie on the floor. He was too heavy.

*Charlie, c'mon, I need you to get up*. But he was nonsensical. I didn't want an image of him like this: a mess on the floor.

I tried to prop him up, to understand the injury to his face. Crushing the need to call someone into a tiny flicker in the back of my mind. Only if it's an emergency. But—trying to hear how the conversation over the phone with whoever this person I would call would go—

"What's wrong?"

"My brother, he's wasted."

"Well,"

"There's blood all over his face and—"

"Did you check for broken bones, punctures, or any bruising?"

"He gets in fights a lot. What if he's got alcohol poisoning?"

"Well—"

*Charlie*—the desperation in my voice alien, for a moment believing there was someone else in the room with us speaking aloud, but no—

*Charlie I can't carry you, you have to get up.*

Panic a winged thing in my chest as he lay there, not moving, splayed. His face smeared. For a moment I thought he was missing his front teeth, but no, there they were. I rubbed my finger along them, wiping the blood on the back of my jeans. Lifting the sides of his shirt, recoiling in case I saw gashes or holes or—but no, just bruises the shapes and colours of storming clouds. Charlie was immobile on the floor, now grimacing or grinning.

*Ben? Ben? 'Zat you?*

Collapsing next to him. *Yeah, Charlie. It's me.*

We hadn't talked in three weeks. Not a word. Just rotated around one another in the way I imagined the large, dark and drifting planet bodies did in the sky, trying to grasp some language that would cross all that space.

*You know, Ben?*

*Know what, Charlie?* Having to lean closer and swallowing my breath at the smell to hear his thready whisper.

*Of course you know, you get it, it's all just*—tongue too thick.

Whisky, I guessed. *No, what Charlie? Know what? What are you talking about?*

*You know it's all just—*

*Just?*

*Just—*

Then nothing.

***

I sat next to him all night. Got a bucket and put garbage bags under him. Made sure he was on his side. Checked again under his shirt and considered his jeans, wasn't embarrassed, then felt a whole slew of unnamed things because I wasn't. Amazed at the weight of a body not alert.

***

I didn't fall asleep. Just listened to the rolling and crashing sound of his breathing all night. Stared at the way light crept and waned and slanted. He didn't get sick on himself. I guess it all just soaked into him, which was new. I remembered how we snuck more beers the night we were first allowed a sip at dinner—when Charlie found out he got into university in the States. Him badgering me when our parents were asleep—*C'mon Ben, Jesus, lighten up*.

We had too much, and he immediately got sick. Behind the tulips. We dug a hole into the earth and covered it up with soil, laughing and swaying. Woolly headed and puffy-eyed the next day, my Dad gleeful and laughing. Mom, unimpressed and muttering, but amusement curving her voice.

***

When morning glinted through the small window, he was awake. We remained silent until the air felt heavy and I said, *Charlie, you can't do that again, you just can't*.

I remember getting up before I could register a reaction, unable to look at him, just grabbing my backpack from my room. Rustling loudly to avoid hearing anything. Returning to throw a blanket on him even though I'd meant to slam out the front door. Placing a glass of water next to him even though I wanted to throw it into the bathtub so it could shatter.

His voice slow and deep, returning from wherever it was he disappeared to those days—

*Okay*.

—

Saskatoon is visible now, rising a corrugated shape out of the flatland. I reach for the map on the dashboard. Full of places I've never been to. I trace their names with my finger. Martensville, Rosthern, Dalmeny, Aberdeen.

"First left," I say.

"Okay."

Charlie drums his thumbs on the steering wheel. He's turned the radio on but it's real quiet. Murmuring. Noise faint enough to fill the background.

I can see a turn-off about eighty metres ahead.

"That one."

Charlie slows the truck down and we tilt sideways in our seats.

Lines of trees stand in makeshift wall dividers separating emptiness. A red farmstead sits faded on our left. Nothing on our right except fields of mustard and Saskatoon staying the same miniature size in the corner of my window until it's gone.

My legs feel cramped. I stretch them, pushing against the floor, clenching the muscles. We've been driving for a while but now that we've turned off the highway, it doesn't feel like we've come far at all.

I look at the map in my hands. Creases neat and sharp. It's a little more worn now, like some I took from the garage and piled under my bed: old maps of Dad's, showing the world as a stretched blue oval, a yellowed sketch of a country with spidered writing; a fake treasure map we drew up once, naming the corners of the garden.

I create a basic map in my mind of what May told us—Alberta

Border, North, Saskatoon, Winter Cold River, Dirt Road.

It's flimsy and curls out of focus when I try and think of where the three houses are sitting.

Did Dill ever say anything? I try and think of a conversation where I ask her about herself. Sound evasive, muffled. Like we're talking underwater. What comes to mind instead is her laughing. Teasing.

*You shouldn't wear shirts so large, Ben. Makes you look younger than you are.*

Smoothing my sleeve in a practiced gesture. Familiar. Deflecting a question with a question.

*Why did you leave Saskatchewan?*

Her shrug, a light lift of her shoulders. *Why not?*

Warm wind through the passenger window makes me think of a night where I found her sitting on the deck, looking someplace far off, eyes out of focus. Pupils dilated.

*What are you thinking about?* I'd asked. A smile enough to obscure her face.

*Oh, the past.* Standing up, brushing grass off her knees, bare next to my face. *Do you want anything to drink? I think I'm going to get some iced tea.*

*No, thanks.*

*Alright.*

Waiting while the sun sank into a red line of fire, the wood deck growing cool under my legs, the moon full and bruised, stars scattered and shining, outlining the garden in shadow. Waiting. Hearing sounds of a truck shuddering off. Charlie coming back from work. Hearing her greet him at the door. Low. Murmured.

I rub my forehead. Look out the window.

"Charlie?"

"Yeah."

"Did—she ever say anything to you about this place?"

Charlie is quiet for a bit. I tap my finger on the door-handle.

"No," he says finally.

"Did you ask?"

He shifts in his seat, stretches his arms against the wheel.

"Yeah. But all she said was that she was from somewhere small." Charlie's voice warms, remembering. "Not much to do there but stare, she said."

He trails off. Mouth drawing into a hard line.

I flip through reels of things Dill might have said. Explicit things. But if I try and think of her talking to me, I just hear *took some of the money* and my mind blanks. If I think of us in the truck coming back from the Royal Tyrrell museum and Charlie glancing at her while she looked out the windshield, all I see is anger on his face.

The seatbelt feels tight across my chest. I shift against the backrest. Charlie drums his fingers on the steering wheel.

"I mean, did she mention anything about her past—I—you two hung out a lot—" I stop abruptly. The back of my neck stinging hot.

Another moment to keep: sitting on my bed, the quilt cold. Staring at her knees, reflected light capping bone. Dill, holding out her hands to take mine. The skin on my back racing.

*Okay, rub your hands together.*

*What?*

Smiling, bringing her hands in front of her nose as if in prayer. *Watch.*

Starting to rub her palms together, the sound reminding me of sandpaper, of the tools in Dimitri's shop. Aware of the sudden need to sweat.

*Okay, now.* Dill leaned forwards and pressed her palms, smooth and heated, against my eyelids. I jerked back a bit.

*Stay still, no don't close your eyes, keep them open.* Her hair against my shoulder. *Just watch.*

Staring into the warm dark of her hands.

Charlie clears his throat. A hawk circles in a slow loop in the distance. It must see a mouse. I scan for a glimmer of water. Nothing. I rub my nose.

"How much did she take, Charlie?"

He moves his hands to the top of the steering wheel and doesn't answer.

"If you see a river turn towards it," I mutter.

More moving fields of watery green, chalk blue sky. Charlie changes gears and the engine roars. It's the loudest sound I've heard in a while and it makes me think of when we got the truck. Before Dill. I was studying *To Kill a Mockingbird* and had been frowning at the pages, absorbed. Charlie had kicked my door in, beaming, dragging me by the wrist outside to the driveway to see its hulk gleaming in the sunset. I was stunned by his excitement, used to constant surliness. Looking at our warped reflections in its side, Charlie a good head taller. *150 horsepower, Ben.*

I remember tilting my head and studying the frayed but sturdy truck, imagining a horde of horses while he talked about its capabilities—thinking they'd be lit from the prairie sunset: blood-orange under a wall of sky. Stars winking bright as their hooves pounded over the plains, dust unfurling in tornado-whorls behind them, necks glistening. Appaloosa chestnut buckskin blue roan palomino—manes flying like war flags, nostrils round black craters, muzzles wet and gleaming silver in the dying daylight. Hearts pounding larger than my fist. I imagined them stopping to look out at the Badlands near Drumheller when Charlie said *All-road terrain*—the eerie cuts into the earth, cliffs of bone-dry dust and cacti in clumps. A golden eagle spiralling above the jagged horizon, its cry dragging through the air, watching. Ford had recently made a commercial like that, I think.

*It's a nice truck, Charlie,* I'd said.

Like the truck had fixed things. Changed things. Like its big presence was enough to counteract the emptiness of our house. But I remember thinking it was still a motor on four wheels that would bring him from A to B, but keep him in Three Hills. It could still topple over if it veered too quickly on a sharp bend in a mountain pass. Or over loose gravel on top of a small road in the empty, criss-cross prairie road grid.

***

I rest my arm on the windowsill to feel air rush over my skin and catch my expression in the side-mirror. The eye-bags and the frown drawing my mouth together surprises me.

I should've kept asking her questions until she answered them. But she must've answered them someway else. Ways I didn't see. Am I just looking for them now? Holding up memories like cards. A year seems a long time, but then, clearly it wasn't. I pinch my eyebrows together. Impressions of the family room bloom in the blood vessels of my eyes. Her hair covering the side of her face. Sitting cross-legged. My hands fidgeting in my lap.

*Do—do you miss home?*

*Sometimes.* Picking at something on her wrist, twisting the skin. Voice tight in her throat. Repeating the word home under her breath, like learning the answer to a joke.

I lean back against the headrest and stare at the coffee stain on the ceiling again. A dark cloud's gone and grown in my chest, settling against my ribcage.

"How did that get up there?"

"Huh?" Charlie glances at me out of the corner of his eye. "Oh. I lost the lid to my go-mug and went too fast over the speed bump at Timmy's. I think I was late getting to work. Wanted to avoid Dimitri's wrath. Ended up getting to work late and covered in coffee."

Charlie gives a low chuckle. He's squinting into the sun. His profile blurs into Dad's—when just me and Dad would drive to a match of Charlie's. The sun'd be pulling down a shade ribboned with blue and red and purple. He'd forget his sunglasses at home so he'd always be squinting out the windshield. We'd always be five minutes late. Mom would be sitting in the stands with her jacket folded across two extra seats, ready with an exasperated look.

*Again, dear?*

Sometimes we'd stop for cheeseburgers and a Coke before. Dad would ask how I was enjoying school and being a moody teen. I'd say, *It's pretty much the same.*

*Thank you for answering my routine parenting questionnaire*, he'd say, miming putting a pen and notebook away. Then he'd tell me to stop being so boring and do something like go to a party, so he could ground me.

I rub my forehead. Pull the seatbelt away from my chest. Let it snap back. The pressure is still there, curled and tight.

"You look a lot like him, you know," I say.

"Like who?"

"Dad."

Charlie's whole body stiffens. I stick my hand out the window and feel the wind resist my open palm. Green blurs out of focus in my periphery. Sunlight reflecting gold-white in every pore on my hand, the edges of my fingers bright red, reminding me of when we'd all outline our flattened hands with red crayon to draw turkeys for Thanksgiving decorations.

I once found a few of those from when me and Charlie were really little. In the garage. Underneath Charlie's history essays. His oddly neat, small handwriting shaping words like *Bismarck* and *Perestroika.*

"Did you know that?" I start picking at the fraying knees of my jeans. "Especially when you squint."

"Ben."

"You also have the same voice. It's weird. Sometimes when you say that you sound just like him."

"Ben—"

"What?" Studying every knit in my jeans. Tiny squares looped with tiny thread.

"—just—shut up about that stuff, okay?"

I pick at the fraying seam along my right leg. "I think you're doing enough shutting up for the both of us." There are faint grass stains that still haven't washed off the shins. A buzzing starts in my ears. My own background radio. Another laugh scrapes out of my throat. "But I'll wait. Whenever it's convenient for you."

He grinds his teeth."What is your problem?"

"What do you think my problem is?"

We pass a line of trees on the left standing dark and solemn. They blur out of sight.

"Ben, can we not do this now?"

His voice straining. The buzzing louder. I let it grow in volume and pretend I didn't hear that note of something in his request. My palms itch. *Dill took some of the money, alright?*

"When else do you want to do it? We'll be driving for a while. I haven't seen a river yet, have you?"

Charlie takes a breath. Inhales. Exhales. Flexes his hands around the steering wheel.

"Well—just—concentrate on looking for one."

I tap my foot in an irregular beat. Nod.

"Sure. Because out here with all of the buildings blocking my view I might miss it, and then where would we be?"

Charlie turns up the radio. Country. I want to laugh. We both hate country. I remember Dill singing Shania Twain loudly in the kitchen once, purposefully badly so we had to cover our ears. I rake my fingers through my hair.

"You are unbelievable."

"Shut the fuck up Ben, I mean it."

I taste something copper in my mouth.

"Fuck you," I say, turning back to the window.

"Hey—watch it—"

"What, only you can say that now?"

"It's disrespectful."

"You're my brother, not my boss."

"Last time I checked I was the adult here."

"I'm not a kid anymore, damnit—"

"Last time I checked, you were."

"I'm almost sixteen, I can get my driver's licence soon for fuck's sake—"

"Like hell that's ever happening—"

"God, you just want to control every fucking thing—"

"That's my fucking job, Ben, to take care of things—"

"I'm not sure if you've noticed, Charlie, but we're sort of in this together, since, you know, both our parents d—"

Charlie slams on the brakes. Wheels shriek and the truck skids to a stop. Dust billows from under the tires, cloaking the windshield in a gold-fire curtain. He unbuckles his seatbelt. It clicks in a sharp staccato. My heart pounds against my ribs, pulsing in my eyes. He turns to face me in his seat, elbow pressed against the steering wheel.

"You want my attention? Okay, you have it. Because I can't drive and listen to you."

I look at the floor. Unbuckle my seatbelt. The buzzing's now a dull roar. I have to get out of the truck.

"What do you want from me, Ben? What do you want me to say?"

I shake my head and whip open the passenger door.

"I don't need to you say anything, Charlie."

"Where the hell do you think you are going?"

"I can't sit and listen to you," I say sarcastically, grass snapping under my soles as I slam the door. Charlie curses and opens and slams his door too.

He stalks around the front of the truck. I'm standing in the dip of grass next to the shoulder. There's no traffic anywhere. Blue surrounds us, an empty stadium.

"Okay, so you're going to be a smart-ass, that's fine—"

"I have your attention now, at least."

An incredulous laugh escapes his mouth.

"Attention? When do you not have my attention?"

I throw my arms in the air, gesturing out to the fields. "Oh, I don't know, every time you ignore what I'm asking you on purpose?"

"Well, I'm not ignoring you now, so c'mon, talk."

We're standing a couple feet apart. My blood's pumping hot and quick. I'm curling my hands tight against my sides. Charlie's changed his stance. Feet shoulder-width apart, staggered.

I clear my throat. "You mean you're going to finally let me mention our parents now? You're even going to let me ask you a question about them and maybe you'll answer?" The wind has picked up; dust salts my eyes. "Just like that? Well, if all it took was not taking your bullshi—"

He moves in a blink. Left fist swings into my face. Spots explode my vision. For a minute I'm stunned. I stagger back, knees buckling. Tangy bitterness fills my mouth. A split lip. I start to laugh, spit. He looks shocked.

I wipe the corner of my mouth against my shoulder. "Yes. Good. Okay."

I bend, launch, and grab him around the waist. He doesn't expect it. I throw my weight into it and pull him to the ground, knock the wind out of him. We crash into the grass and it scratches my bare arms. I raise my fist and smash his nose, twice. He throws me off. My shoulder lands hard against the ground. I scrabble back up. Charlie's already on his feet. We slam into one another again, arms locked around each other in a vice grip. I see grey cotton shirt and horizon and earth. We fall down again and the air's knocked out of me. I'm pounding my fists into his ribs. He's pummelled my abdomen, jaw, back. Every fist a hammer-blow. Elbows are hitting arms and legs and faces. I hear a crack and don't know who it's from.

It goes on until we're breathing ragged, until blood's falling down my chin. I feel it dripping from my swollen nose. My arms are going leaden. Adrenaline's made my heart erratic. Breaths rip out of me in gasps. I clench my body and swing my knee into his side. He grunts.

"I can't walk around like they never existed, Charlie—"

He goes still. I roll him over, my arms straining against his bodyweight, and sit on his chest, my knees pinning his wrists into the ground. His hands curl palms up bruised and split towards the sky. His eyes are unfocused. Blood runs down his face from a cut under his hairline.

"—because they're still here, Charlie—" I hit my forehead with my hand, twice, spots exploding in my eyes, "—all the goddamn time. They're never not. What do you expect from me? Huh? To forget? To shut up? What do you want from me?"

I grab the front of his shirt and shake him. He doesn't struggle or move, just lays there limp.

"C'mon. Say something."

I shake him again.

He coughs. "Fine. You want to talk about Dad?"

His voice odd, reminding me of still water. Calm. Flat. Without letting go of his shirt, I wipe the side of my face into my shoulder.

"Yeah. Sure. Okay."

I twist my fingers tighter in the fabric of his shirt, his chest moving up and down in rapid successions.

"You want to take a trip down memory lane? All the way? Or do you just want to keep it like you remember?"

I lean my knees into his wrists. He doesn't move. I jut my chin into his face.

"Okay. Banff. You want to know why we went to Banff? Without Dad?"

The wind, every stalk of grass, shifts. Like a crowd hidden, waiting. My whole body aches. His lips curl. He coughs. Twice. A laugh. He starts laughing. It shudders through his body.

"He was with someone else."

A high-pitched ringing begins in my ears. I feel it in the stem in of my spine, every vein.

"What?"

"But she forgave him."

Tears are leaking out of his eyes. I watch them roll slow, drip out of sight.

"What?"

"Forgave him. It was just the once, he said. A mistake. I heard them. They didn't see me."

His whole body shaking with laughter now. I feel his ribs strain against my legs.

"It was a long time ago. Years. But it's all I can think about when I think of him now. The only goddamn thing."

Something's burning in my gut, my vision blurs; his face unfocused. I struggle to see it. His hair keeps looking grey in the white sun. Charlie coughs again. Blood and spit bubble at the corner of his mouth.

"Especially—especially since he was the one driving too fast."

I stare into the blackness of his eyes, my face warped in them, blurred by a shivering film of water. I'm shaking. Teeth rattling.

My fist collides with his face. It doesn't break his laugh.

I do it again and again. He lets me.

***

Clouds gather in piles, slow and purposeful. I watch them trek across the sky, moved by an invisible force, every motion carving new edges into their sides. They are towers of marble dust, heaving sea waves.

We're still lying in the grassy dip next to the road. No cars have come or gone. The ground digs into my back. I'm sprouting out of it. I watch the line of my ribs rise and fall under my shirt, covered in dirt and grass and bloodstains. I hear a meadowlark sing before its notes are carried off in the wind.

"Let's go," Charlie says.

I don't move. I concentrate on the sharp and itchy grass poking into my skin. Every rock and ridge. Charlie struggles to his knees, hacks, wipes his nose a bit, then winces. Staggers to his feet.

"C'mon, Ben."

The sun on its way down throws Charlie's shadow over me, edging his hair in light, covering the mess of his face.

He holds his hand out to me. I grab it.

***

We drive until the sun sinks orange to the horizon, passing some old railroad tracks that disappear rusted into the grass. Trees grow thicker, taller, the land wilder. Sloughs glint metal bright and scatter along the fields in clumps. I get out beef jerky from the glove compartment. It's too painful to chew so I suck on it instead. Charlie shakes his head when I offer him some.

He pulls the truck off into the grass next to the road. We set up our sleeping bags in the bed of the truck. When I hold up the unassembled tent, Charlie looks at it with a blank expression. I shrug, tossing it.

Stars glimmer, peeking out from the canopy of darkening red. I can see the shrouded Milky Way dashed across the sky. Venus a steady light. As the air cools it smells of a darker green, feeling skin smooth on my face.

It's a struggle to get to my knees. Charlie slumps instead. The truck shudders under us, shifts. I hiss when I bend to unzip the sleeping bag. It's too much effort to open all the way.

I lie down. Charlie doesn't get in his sleeping bag. Lays on top. The material whispers against his jeans.

I think I hear a faint howling but it's gone. The sky is massive and presses down in a magnetic pull. I let it all fill my irises, imprinting it there.

"She only took what she put in."

I turn to see him. He's staring at the sky.

"I don't know why she didn't say anything. Not about the money. That's not—that doesn't—but about anything." He looks at me, bruises starting on his face.

"Maybe it was too hard to talk about," I say.

Charlie holds my gaze.

It is quiet. Real quiet.

I shift in my sleeping bag to look again at the million pinpricks of starlight, when all of a sudden, drifting in a slow spiral out of the dark, a wavering curtain of electric green threaded with bright blue and tips of purple appears—moving across the sky like thousands of silk ribbons.

My breath catches as I watch the northern lights dance. Charlie's still, and I know he's watching them too.

"Charlie?"

"Yeah."

"Do—do you have a favourite memory of them?"

Charlie doesn't answer for a bit. I pick at my sleeping bag.

"There are too many," he says, finally.

My throat feels thick and I swallow. Charlie's breathing is slow and ragged. I keep my breaths shallow.

We drift.

It is your right to keep some answers to yourself. Especially this sort of *why*. Everything packed and it all fits into one bag. Still, even after a year. Placing the baseball bat under the seat next to you so it's hidden but you know you can twist and reach it in seconds. Having practiced this move until your back ached. Having performed it, too.

You've allowed yourself to cry this time. Having tried once not to and realizing it just built into you like a corrosive poison that made things difficult to manage. Knowing now, as soon as you felt it—that pressure—to let it go. Down your face and neck. Driving into the sun and everything alight and vivid from that unleashing. Rolling the windows down no matter the temperature; needing air, always.

Now though, heat only lay dormant for the night but was fast to rise. By ten in the morning the sun hot enough to make sweat between your breasts, under your knees. *How are...?* But you shelve the thought quickly, mapping out the road: straight and straight until the turn and the river and then left. Seeing other faces now in your mind—some of the faces you saw every night, especially when things were good. And they'd been good a lot, lately. Enough so that guilt, that many clawed creature, would clutch and clutch as you wondered, *how are...?*

You are only one person. When you were discovering the itch under your feet to be anywhere else, the old woman with the long braid down her back gripped your hands and said, *There is a lot that only one woman can do*. For the rest of your years since, you saw how that sentence could mould itself, could be a blessing; a curse. But it was a truth.

As you shift gears, passing others daringly, the relentless creature continues—*how are they, have they noticed?* Because you can't help it: seeing a slope of broad shoulders, a mess of hair behind a book.

You have realized there is something selfish about loving people. To want and ask and want. To want someone to want. To access a portal into another person, visibility into what's hidden, sharing your own—you've craved that since you grew teeth. Since starting a life pattern of getting into different beige and grey cars every five then three then two years until you were sixteen and could say, fuck it. Could drive, could run. Didn't have to prepare for more flaking doors and porches or colourful doors and plain porches. To prepare for strangers who you could always read first. Relieved, now, to see people's wishes naked on their faces, but at the time resentful, mistrustful. Tired. Now knowing this awareness as a gift. Yours.

Like when you stood and stared and stared at him in the living room. Noticing everything. Hearing fingers worrying into couch fabric. Staring right into yourself and yourself staring back: the naked want. And the simplicity of it: *You can stay as long as you want.*

But what if I go?

What then?

You know motion is life. You've seen what happens when someone is forced into inertia, kept in a place without freedom, without wind and open horizon. Having tried to recognize such a person, knowing you shared blood. Her teeth and hair and eyes the same as yours. But she was dissolving entirely—into memory, a picture in the newspaper. You vowed to yourself you would not be her, ever. Anger awakened in you like lightning a fire, because you knew how history had unfolded to that moment in that room with the grey smell and fluorescent bulb. The woman dissolving right into the air in front of you with no one left to wonder—*but how is...?* Your anger physical; grateful for every muscle that helped you to stand and leave. Knowing with certainty when the man in the uniform said, *Time's up*, you would never see this woman again. You wouldn't.

But you would. Sometimes when you were between places; when you were crammed into a gas station bathroom with a small bar of soap washing the dust from your face and fingers and armpits you would glance at the mirror and there she would be in the startle of the eyebrow, the curve at the mouth. Rattled, you would pull your shirt back on, propel into your car and the night and drive and drive. You got to see a lot this way. You met gangs of bikers travelling to California, who were Vietnam vets and said how they had seen the northern lights in the Yukon and salmon spawning in B.C. You met hippies with dreadlocks and hemp shirts and battered guitars who were drifting to find understanding and to see where the road took them. You met women with piercings who kissed each other with tongues right on the highway. You met visitors from all over the continent and sometimes from across the seas in camper vans or tour buses who were incredulous at the landscape.

*It's so vast, so beautiful, so stark, what a country, hardly anyone.*

You saw people who saw you with recognition. But you kept going, scared of that familiarity. Not yet, you told them silently, and they understood; they were also in-between places.

But when the car finally broke down and you found two boys who looked at you the way you looked at others—how you all wanted the same thing—to take something back—to reverse it all and have someone lost come back—

You started to crave looking into the mirror and searching for the similarities of her in your face. Daring to think of the word for her you hadn't thought of, not in a long time. Tracing heavy curves of those letters into the mirror after a shower; letters shaped like hills and mountains and one as round as the world—

Once, as a little girl, you thought of loneliness as something romantic—an image from a black and white movie. A woman in a patterned dress, tapered at the shoulders and waist, standing on a train platform in the middle of nowhere—the mid-west U.S., or middle provinces here—creating a fan of shade over her face. Not sure if she was arriving or watching someone go. But waiting, certainly. Just standing there with a dress not meant for all that dust, and no one there. Just her, waiting.

Was there anticipation? Expectation? Understanding? She just kept standing there, shadow obscuring her face. You felt this embarrassed burn in the back of your throat for her because she looked so foolish. *Do something,* you remember whispering. But then she started to rise on her tiptoes, a cord of muscle tautening along her calves. Her other arm floated up to signal an arrival in the distance, maybe. Her whole being starting to shine and shine and you knew it didn't matter what that arrival meant at all because opportunity was coming and she was ready.

No, you realized later. Loneliness is just this sweater we all have and think we can get rid of, but it's still there, in our closet. We put it on without thinking, or because it suits us. Because we know how we stand in it.

Scrubbing and scrubbing your arms with a tiny bar of borrowed motel soap over a chipped gas station bathroom sink—you thought that was loneliness, but it wasn't. It was when you looked across the table under that naked lightbulb at your mom; when Charlie looked at you in the living room; when you sat cross-legged across from Ben, surrounded by books and memories piled and piled.

Loneliness: a fabric that can be machine washed. That's children safe. All around available. Run of the mill, honestly. Nothing noteworthy or particular about it.

But wanting—wanting people to want. That was something to be pulled out of you. By the roots. To get in the car and drive and drive until you found the strength in you to tear the last of it out.

—

When we get up, we lay for a bit just looking at the sky. Clouds smeared like the underside of a wave, fringed in morning light. Everywhere, stiff. I feel my split lip and know my left eye is swollen. Grunting to I finally sit up. Charlie's face is entirely purple on one side, blood crusted around his nose and mouth. I grab onto the truck to stand. Charlie does the same. For a moment we just stare out over the fields and trees at the emptiness of the road and land that goes on and on. We watch the sun rise with arms of orange and pink and red over the rim of the horizon turning the clouds violet. A picture that knocks the wind out of you.

Getting out of the truck bed makes me grit my teeth; my legs refuse to bend. Sleeping without the tent was probably unwise. Charlie helps me vault down. I stumble as my knees buckle. He pats me on the back.

The truck is warm when we get it in. Charlie turns on the engine and it rumbles under us.

"So—" he starts.

"Yeah."

"Keep going?" He looks at me.

I nod, unblinking.

"Okay."

We pull from the side of the road.

Silence settles comfortably. I open my window a bit and hear air rushing over the glass, smelling cool earth. The clouds are drifting leviathans. I study their contours, memorize their shape.

Something glimmers in my periphery. A flicker of silver. I lean to look ahead. Water. A dusty turn-off hides behind long grass.

"Charlie."

"What?"

"Slow down."

"Okay."

"Turn, turn."

We veer right and pebbles sound under the tires, the back of the truck swerving. We're facing a tiny road. Unpaved. There is a small ribbon of a river on our left. Reeds bow and bend in the breeze, lining the sides. It races ahead into the sun.

"Charlie—"

"Yeah."

I feel tingling in my feet and hands. The bruises and cuts twinge, but it's a good feeling.

He revs the gas. The back of the truck fishtails again. He presses lighter, keeps a measured speed, and grips the wheel tightly. Loose gravel covers the road. I can see dust rising behind the truck in the rear-view mirror.

As we move, following the river, I can't help but wonder what it was they were talking about in the car that day. Charlie's graduation, bills? Maybe they were talking about what would be for dinner. Or about something that parents talk about in privacy, about memories only they share. Their lives before kids. B.C., as Dad used to say.

I am glad I don't know what it was. That it happened fast. *Instantly*, Jimmy said. Maybe it happened too fast for fear and they were thinking about all of us on the couch, laughing. Maybe that's what they saw before it all stopped.

Gravel scatters and bursts under the tires.

I allow myself to really think of them as I would in my room every night right after it happened. I'd lay on my back across the quilt on my bed—the only old thing in our house—my Mom's Mom's—someone never mentioned at dinner and even Charlie couldn't unturn photographic evidence of her—and mentally sketch the slope of Dad leaning against my bookshelves as he talked about work, which I didn't really understand; something to do with engineering. Fascinating only to me now. The crinkles at the edges of his eyes, his habit of pressing his glasses against the bridge of his nose, catching the glare from my desk lamp. He had a slight stoop and sometimes smelled of a stolen cigarette. Inhaling now I can almost smell it—tar and vanilla. At first I went to the closest gas station to try and see if I could guess which pack it was until the attendant chased me away for being underage and *just damn depressing, son.*

I have to push my feet into the floor and grip the truck's door handle against the ache. Never having wanted something so badly in my life—to reach out and touch the knee of his worn jeans, for his knuckles to graze my hair. A want that scared me—that had teeth. For Mom to barge in without knocking—an increasingly embarrassing thing I discovered as every year lapped by. But always unapologetic, her sharp laughter when I wasn't even doing anything except *reading, again? And not that Salinger? Really, Ben, maybe try something less typically teen or written by a woman.* Intrigued by these memories—learning about your parents—who they were before becoming Parents.

*You know, like Flannery O'Connor or Louise Erdrich or how about that Margaret Atwood*—carving the names into me for later, already seeing my hands picking the books off the library shelf, ready to devour them and find words my Mom found interesting. *At least you fold your sweaters, can't say the same for your brother*—raising her voice at the end so Charlie, across the hall, could hear, her oncoming laughter apparent.

Even now with the wind through the truck window, I can hear the sides of her mouth raising, remembering how when she sat at my desk chair, the lamp on my nightstand lit streaks of red in her hair. And Charlie, able to perfect annoyance since he started high school, shouting back, *They'll get dirty, what's the point?*

Except that ever since it happened, he folds everything meticulously, everything all just so.

A hill rises like a wave out of the ground and the river darts away. I dig my fists into my eyes and swallow.

***

As we move closer towards the hill, there they are, over a crest: three houses. Brown and square against the golden grass, barbwire fence taught around the perimeter. I hear Charlie take a sharp breath.

I see them, too. The piles of stones in the shape of men with their arms held out.

Charlie speeds up a little. I'm gripping the knees of my jeans.

When we pull up to the fence, my lungs are fit to burst. Charlie turns off the truck. For a moment we just sit and stare at the houses. The light is all gold and blue, falling in shades through spaces in the clouds. There's a clump of trees just behind the houses; the rest of the land a scraped bowl. We get out of the truck. The wind has picked up and rakes through the grass, which bows, gleaming white. I feel like something's hooked onto my shoulders, pulling me forwards.

From outside the truck the houses look shabbier. Fierce. Patched and held up with metal shingles of different sizes and shapes on the roofs, the houses all leaning sideways a little. I can see piles of wood stacked next to the nearest one, a shining axe blade driven into a standing wood block. Dogs start to bark, the sound jagged in the wind.

Me and Charlie look at one another. I know we are a sorry mess. The side of Charlie's mouth tilts a little, stretching a cut. I give him a tight grin back, which makes my cheek ache. We duck under the fence.

***

As we move over the grass, I can see a dark shape heading towards us. A boy in a shirt three sizes too big and pants cinched with a giant belt, skate shoes with loose laces. A shock of blue hair. I can see his glare from here and put my hands in my pockets.

We slow our pace and stagger so we're not walking directly side by side. But we don't stop. When a couple of metres separate us, I can feel goosebumps start across my arms.

Up close I can tell the kid's barely fourteen, but there's an old look to him. It's the flatness in his eyes. They don't reflect the light, but absorb it. Like Charlie's after it happened.

"Who are you?" He crosses his arms, expression severe.

There's a small circle scar on one of his forearms, like a cigarette burn. His arms are skinny. Something about his eyes remind me of Dill's, but his mouth is longer, thinner. Another faint scar, a thin one, splits his eyebrow; a scythe-shaped one jagged near his mouth.

I move my hand as if to hold it out but jerk it back. The kid still hasn't uncrossed his arms.

"I'm Ben."

"Charlie."

"What do you want?"

I clear my throat. "We're looking for—for Dill."

His expression never changes.

"She tell you to come?"

"Yes."

The kid furrows his eyebrows and stares at us outright. Looks me up and down and then Charlie, narrowing his eyes. Then he uncrosses his arms and turns around abruptly, starting back towards the houses. Me and Charlie don't move for a moment and shoot each other an unsure glance.

"C'mon," the kid says, his voice sharp, cutting through wind and grass.

We all start to traipse up the knoll and when we get level with the stones, I can't help but stare at them, throwing scarecrow-like shadows along the hill, no higher than our knees. Every stone thin, slate grey, and piled carefully. I feel them watch us pass, sightless, as we move up to the door of the house closest to us. When we get behind them they look like the last soldiers standing, walking out into a vast world unknown and unforgiving. But their arms are held out wide, gathering it all in an embrace.

The dogs we heard barking have stopped. I hear chains rattling and the sounds of boots on dirt. A door slams. I know instinctively we are not going to meet anyone in the other houses.

I peer at the stacked wood and smell pine. The axe is driven far into the block, its red painted handle peeling. There's a fire pit and jerry cans. Some old blankets are thrown against the side of the house next to three green plastic deck chairs. The kid stands at the door and knocks, once. It shudders under his fist. I think I see the half-moon of a face behind a curtain before it flutters shut.

Charlie moves to stand close behind me. An old woman opens the door. Her face dry and wrinkled like sand, hair long, white, and braided to her waist. The way her mouth purses, I don't think she has any teeth. She immediately steps away, back into the shadows of the house without a sound.

The kid doesn't say anything and moves inside.

Me and Charlie follow and the door shrieks as it shuts behind us.

Too small, suffocating. I think of all the emptiness that surrounds the house and feel like I'm on a raft in the middle of a sea. Me and Charlie take a few awkward steps in.

There is little furniture. A sagging yellow couch pushes up against the far wall and a couple of chairs with the stuffing coming out are clustered around it. All of them are old and held together with duct tape. There is a small circular wooden table with matching chairs. Some of the backs are missing spokes, rope knotted in their place. I smell a faint medicinal smell and woodsmoke. Fishing poles and a hunting rifle lean next to the door.

Hanging above the couch is a huge tapestry, so large it pools at the floor. It is woven with fabric in vivid shades of blue-green, dotted with beads—a roiling landscape I don't understand. The ceiling light is a stained yellow glass bulb. A small bookshelf crammed by the door holds an assortment of things: old books with tattered spines; antlers; a beautifully carved box; crayons; broken toys; gutting and carving knives; sweaters and boots and toques and mitts.

I feel like I'm staring too openly and turn away. Light's coming from an ajar door at the end of the room, a tiny golden triangle reflected on the floor. The kid's gone inside. I hear murmuring.

Charlie lightly rocks on his heels, his head only a few feet from the ceiling. He keeps his arms at his sides as if to shrink in.

Sweat gathers in my palms. The old woman still doesn't say anything. She's sitting in one of the chairs by the entranceway, looking out the window even though the curtains are closed.

Charlie's studying the kitchen: a small burner stove with some cupboards and pots piled on a counter; freezer humming from a generator. I rub against pressure in my chest.

"Hello." The voice a wisp, faint.

We turn. A girl in a faded flannel nightgown appears; the kid standing behind her. There are circles under her eyes, which are grey. Her hair is dark like Dill's, angled sharply to her chin, cheekbones smooth and round.

"You must be them. The ones Dill stays with." She looks us up and down, carefully, like she's memorizing the look of us.

I nod jerkily. The boy is holding onto her arms, helping her move slowly into the room.

"Tim, get them a glass of water. They're friends of Dill and they've come a long way."

He scowls. "Fine. But you have to lie down."

"On the couch," she commands.

It takes a few minutes, Tim supporting her carefully. Her eyes are drawn shut in a wince. When he helps lower her to the couch, she lets out a wet cough that sounds like a soaked sponge hitting pavement.

Tim goes and gets cups, each one different. Two are large plastic ones from the movie theatres, the images on their sides old. He also gets a mug that reads "Vancouver Island," a totem pole behind the words. There is a camping cooler of water on the kitchen counter. He pours quickly and pushes ours into our hands, carefully taking the mug to her.

"Please sit," she says.

We pull the wooden chairs from the circular table to the couch.

"We have some cheese and crackers if you're hungry," she offers.

"No, I'm okay, thank you," I say.

Charlie clears his throat.

"I'm good too, thank you."

I take a gulp of the water. It tastes a little of soil. It's cold though and goes right through my ribs. Charlie absently runs his thumb along the lip of the cup.

She lifts the mug slowly, the kid watching her the whole time, eyes creased dark underneath. I start picking at the knees of my jeans. Charlie jiggles his leg then stops. Water sloshes onto his pants. He absently brushes at it and then just rests his hand flat on his thigh.

"Dill found out I'd gotten a bit worse. Tim sent her a letter." The girl looks at the kid but not angrily. He rubs his forehead with a fist. "I didn't know what else to do."

She lays a hand on his arm. A huge bruise stretches from her knuckles to wrist. It looks like a purple sun. I flex my hands over my knees.

Tim swipes angrily at his face before getting up. He goes to gently lay a blanket on the old woman's lap; she's statue-still.

The wood and rope of the chair are digging into my back. Charlie's knee starts jittering up and down again.

"She's very kind, Dill. Takes care of people. Sometimes when it's not her burden."

I meet her gaze.

Charlie stands. It's abrupt. His chair tilts backwards for a moment, suspended. It rocks on its feet awkwardly before settling again with a thump. Standing he looks giant. The old woman gives a small cough. He curls and uncurls his hands.

"I'm sorry we troubled you. We shouldn't've—it was—come on, Ben."

I rise to my feet.

Her face full of something. I'm trying not to look at her knee bones. She motions for Tim to help her stand. The light in the house is muted and warm. She moves slowly forward, holding tightly to Tim, his arms around her back, hands clasped underneath hers—like they're about to start dancing. She's not taken her eyes off me and Charlie.

"She was going to stay. But there's nothing here for her. I told her that once. That you have to take your opportunities. It's not all on you, I said. I wanted her to go as far as she could."

She looks exhausted, Tim now mostly supporting her weight. As he pulls her across the room she bends her long neck to keep staring intensely. I recognize the expression as one of Dill's. Something on our faces makes her laugh. Her voice floats through the small house.

"She's gone back. Left saying she had to go so you wouldn't worry."

***

When we get to the truck the wind has picked up into a howl. It tears through the long grass, sets the clouds clamouring, gathering for a run.

We race them home.

—

And soon, we are there. The slow reel of the main road: the gas stations and DQ and Super 8 and the college. We see Dimitri leaving May's café. He stops to nod. Charlie dips his head in return. Butter seeps through the paper bag Dimitri is holding. Hunger startles awake in my gut.

I see it a little now, I think, what Charlie sees when he looks at this place. How small it is, everything just so. But I'm OK with it. Charlie's always been halfway out of here and I get that. But. The relief when we turn into our driveway. Charlie shuts off the engine and we take a moment to appreciate the peeling garage door.

And there—light glinting off the hood, her long hair swinging over her shoulder. I open the door, Charlie already out of the truck. The slope of the driveway raising her; the sense of tipping our heads. She shifts so we are all standing eye to eye to eye. Looking and also not looking. All the relief just to see her, a new energy thrumming from her.

"Okay," she says.

Our faces, giving it all away.

THE END

# ACKNOWLEDGMENTS

It goes without saying:

This book wouldn't have been possible without the steadfast support and encouragement from many dear friends, family, and teachers over the years. I'd first like to thank the gorgeous-hearted group of bright, talented people I was blessed to have had for my writing workshop in Edinburgh, who got the flame of this alight—Dan, Rebecca, Dani, Maria, Ross, Bennett, Lianna, Richard; I was lucky. And of course, some of my professors: Dr. Allyson Stack, who showed me good editing, and so too, good writing; Alan Warner, for being so generous with his wisdom, time, and good humour. The lifelong friends I got to meet: Cailey, Kimber, Kyley (the Square!)—you know. May we reunite to camp in a trailer on a beach in the south of France again someday soon. Or picnic in Edinburgh's spellbinding Meadows, where the first few pages of this book was written.

Thank you to the entire Stevens family for reading this wee novel with care many years ago, and for wanting to know more—Brendan, for your encouragement when I was first applying to MFA programs; J, for still believing in my writing progress and inviting me out into fresh, creative waters. May I meet you out there again, someday. Meghan, for being one of my OG writing champions and a fellow Fanfic fanatic at an early age—that's the stuff of origin myths right there. Taylor, for contest-winning feedback and always, great conversation. I'd also like to deeply thank Rosemary Nixon, for reigniting my love of writing and reading (and therefore rewriting and rereading) after a long, long, dry spell. Caitlynn, for immediately welcoming me into Calgary's thriving literary scene, for being my first reader when I was back across the pond, a port of Scottish literary kinship after Edinburgh, and who has since become a dear friend (you too, Brandon!). There is truly an exhaustive list of YYC folks I hope to thank each individually in some small way at some point. This city! I must also give a shout-out to Dr. Christina Luckyj, Dr. Jason Haslam, and Ms. Harrison (Ingrid) for being inspiring, talented teachers of the written word (and generous references).

To the wonderful women of Stonehouse who gave the story of Ben, Charlie, and Dill actual, real pages (and me) a chance—a thousand times, thank you. You are incredibly supportive and true champions of your authors. I'm over the moon to have my first book printed by this small but fierce indie press. And Silvia: my best cheerleader, friend—blessed to know you. I must thank FreeF*all* (Ryan, Crystal) for bringing us together. (So too, I must heartily thank Yardarm, for the fabulous cocktails which provided me liquid courage to submit this thing…)

And, finally: my parents. I couldn't have done any of this without you—my love and appreciation for you both goes beyond what I can convey. All I have, as always, are words. So thank you, thank you. I love you.